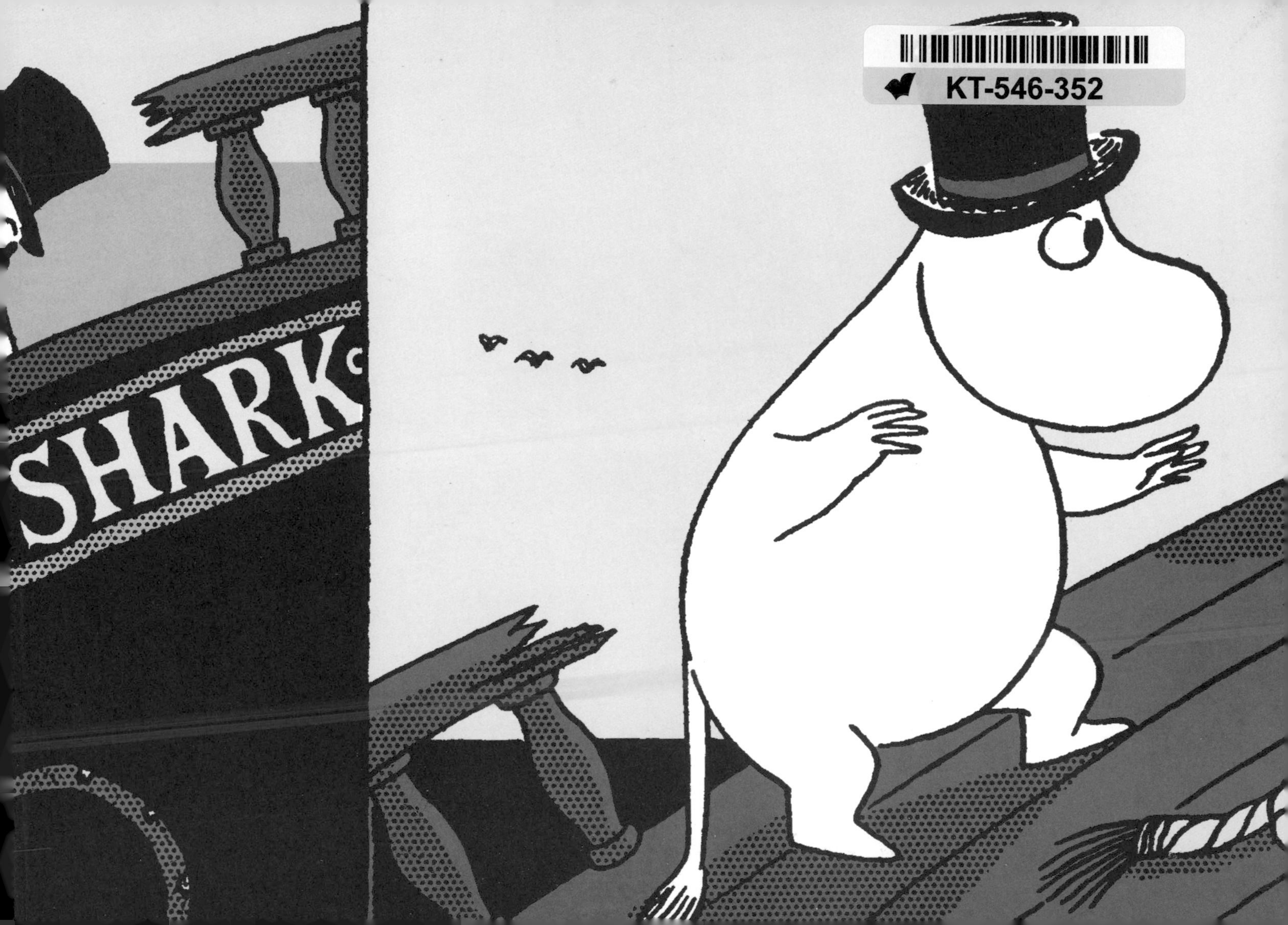
SHARK

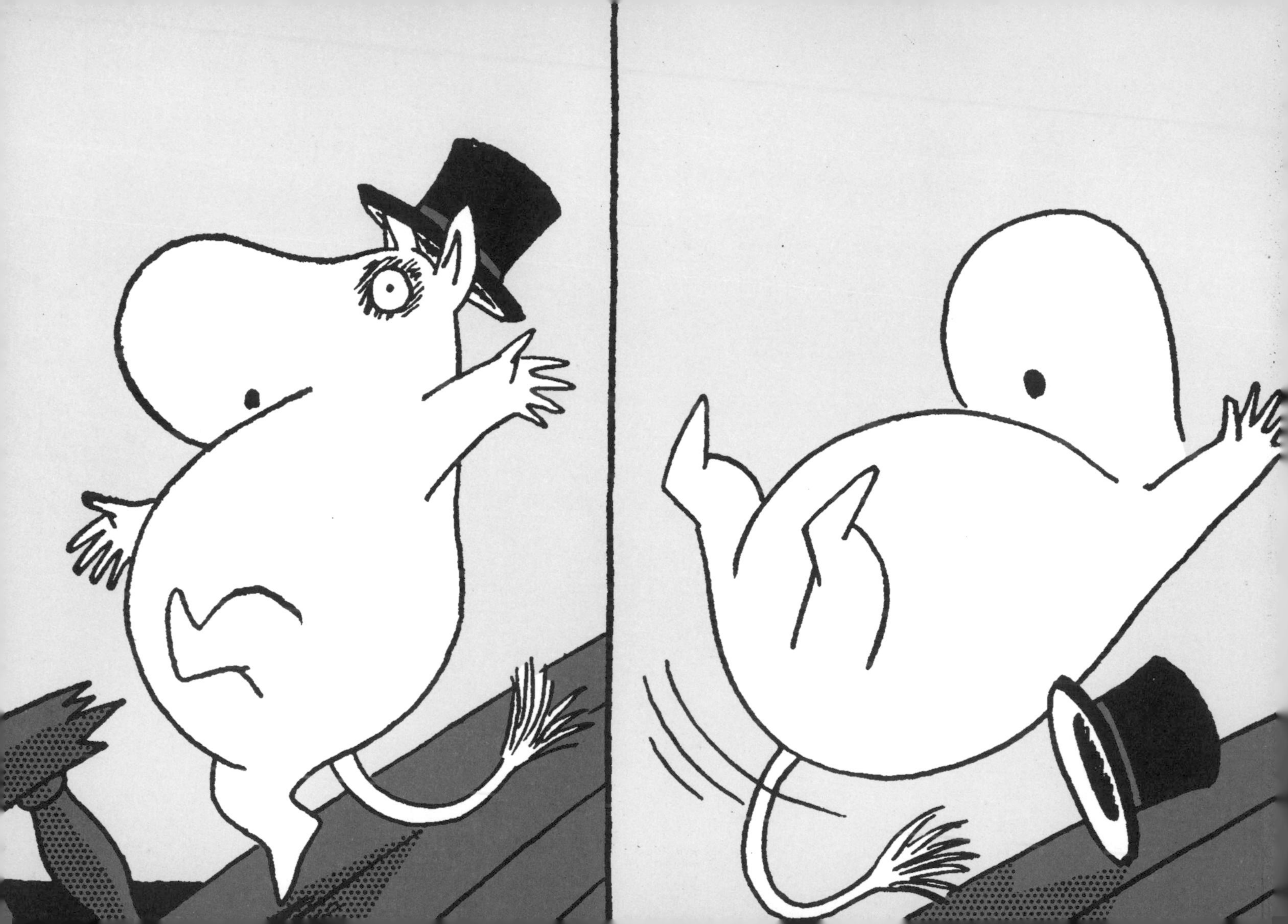

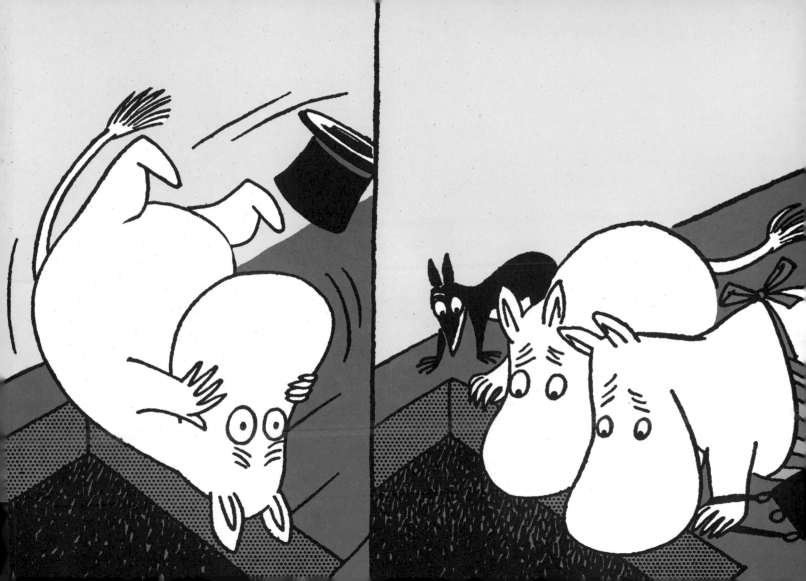

Enfant is an imprint of Drawn & Quarterly.

www.drawnandquarterly.com

First edition: November 2013.
Printed in Malaysia.
10 9 8 7 6 5 4 3 2 1

Library and Archives Canada Cataloguing in Publication
Jansson, Tove, artist
Moomin's Desert Island / Tove Jansson.
Originally published in Evening News, London, [1955].
ISBN 978-1-77046-134-5 (pbk.)
1. Graphic novels. I. Title.
PZ7.7.J35Mod 2013 j741.5'94897
C2013-902362-3

Distributed in the USA by:
Farrar, Straus and Giroux
Orders: 888.330.8477

Distributed in Canada by:
Raincoast Books
Orders: 800.663.5714

Distributed in the United Kingdom by:
Publishers Group UK
info@pguk.co.uk

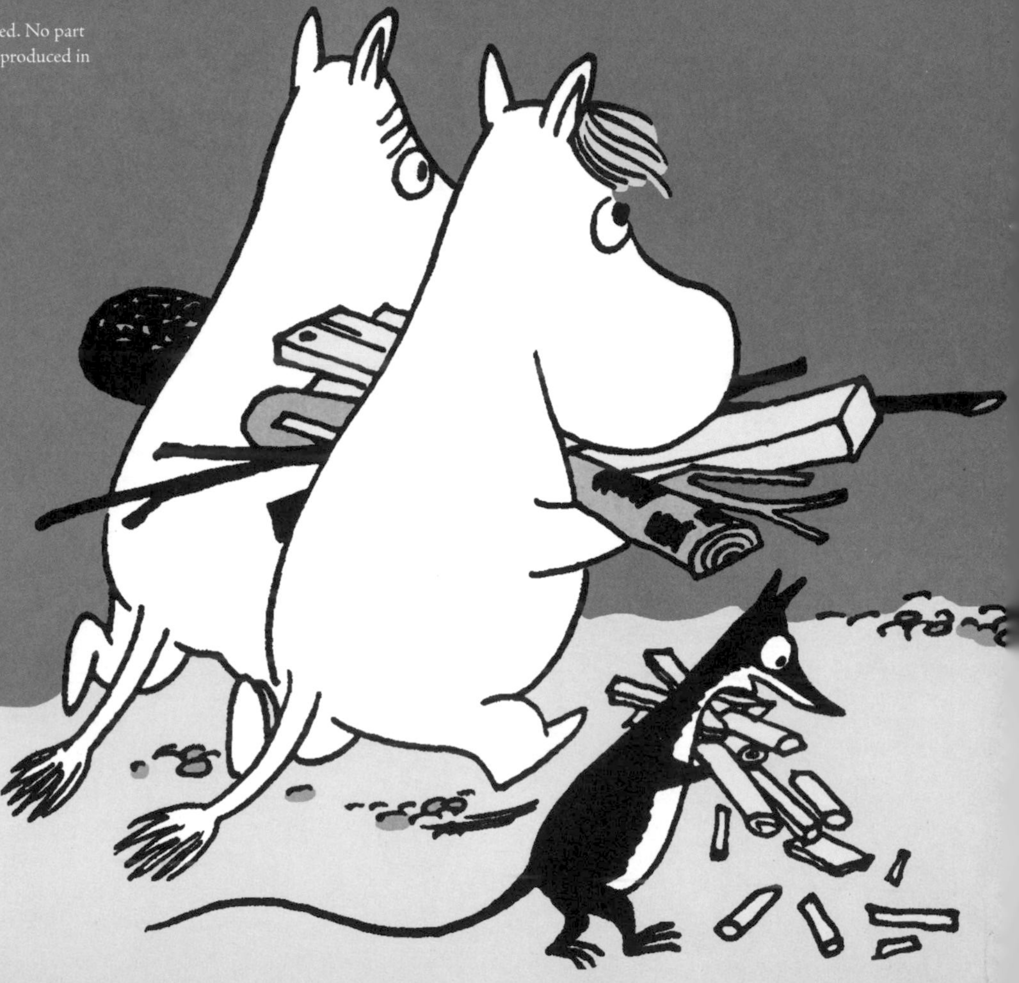

MOOMIN'S DESERT ISLAND

Tove Jansson

ENFANT

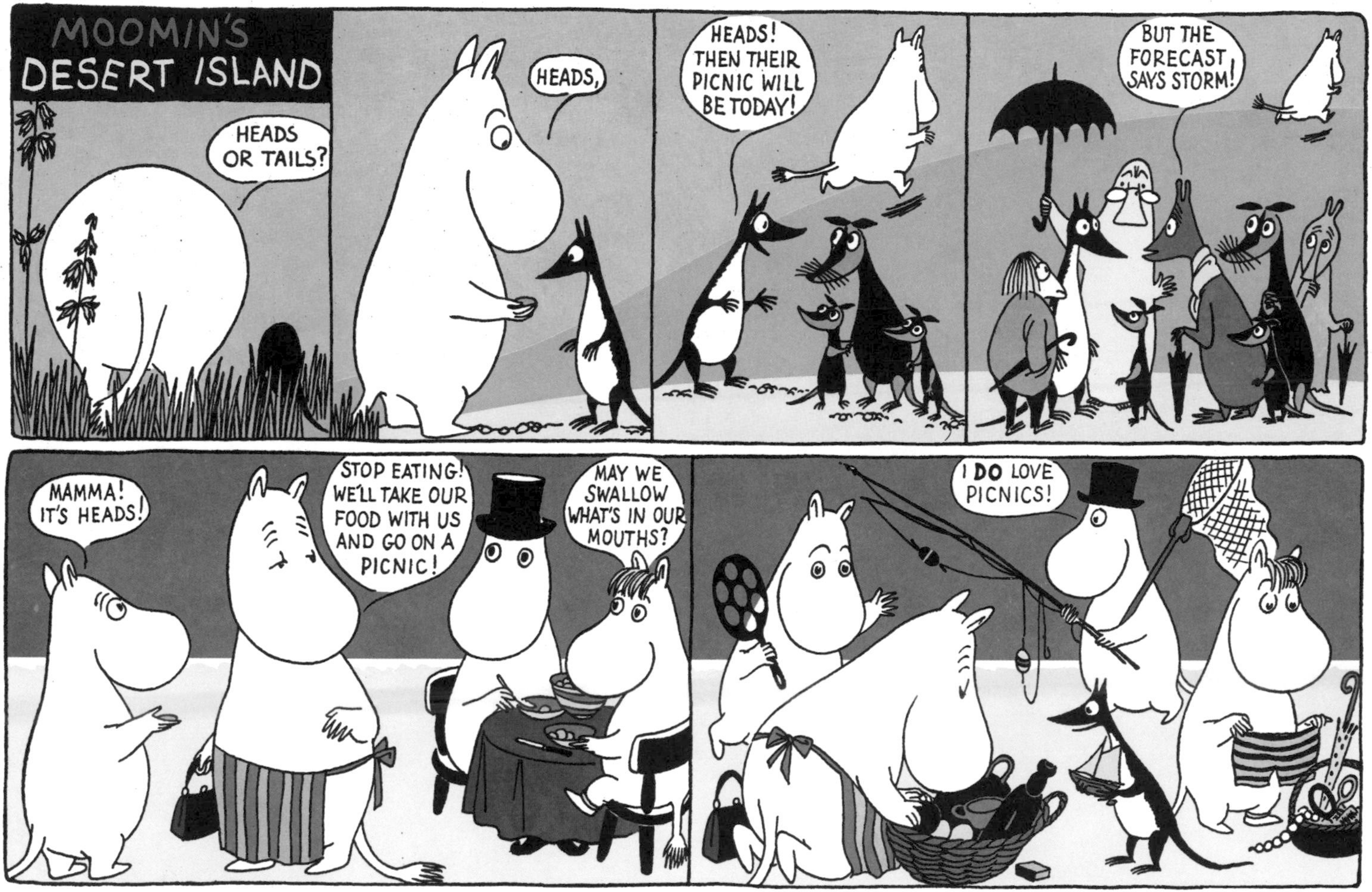
MOOMIN'S DESERT ISLAND
HEADS OR TAILS?
HEADS,
HEADS! THEN THEIR PICNIC WILL BE TODAY!
BUT THE FORECAST SAYS STORM!
MAMMA! IT'S HEADS!
STOP EATING! WE'LL TAKE OUR FOOD WITH US AND GO ON A PICNIC!
MAY WE SWALLOW WHAT'S IN OUR MOUTHS?
I **DO** LOVE PICNICS!

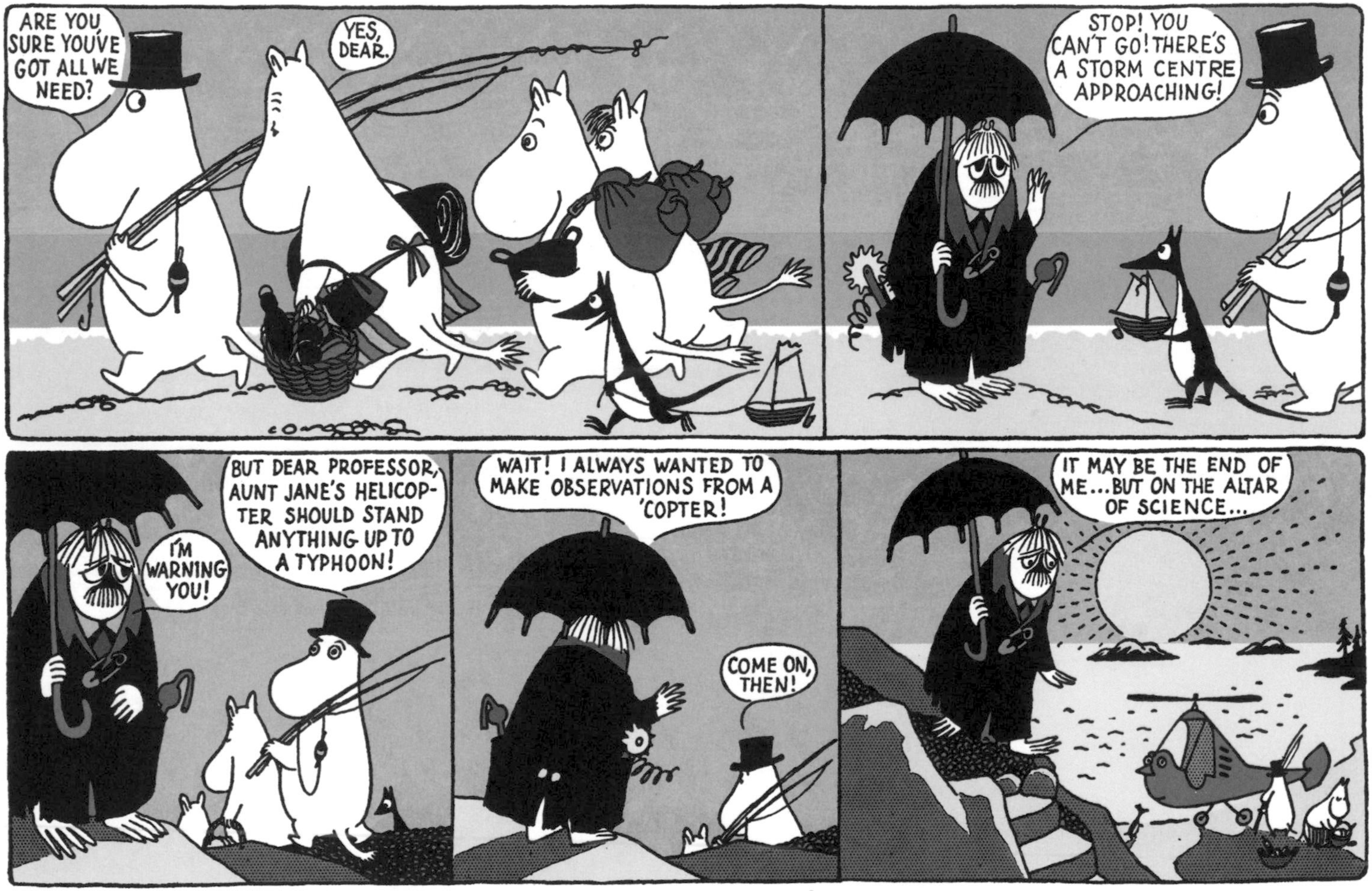
ARE YOU SURE YOU'VE GOT ALL WE NEED?
YES, DEAR.
STOP! YOU CAN'T GO! THERE'S A STORM CENTRE APPROACHING!
I'M WARNING YOU!
BUT DEAR PROFESSOR, AUNT JANE'S HELICOPTER SHOULD STAND ANYTHING UP TO A TYPHOON!
WAIT! I ALWAYS WANTED TO MAKE OBSERVATIONS FROM A 'COPTER!
COME ON, THEN!
IT MAY BE THE END OF ME...BUT ON THE ALTAR OF SCIENCE...

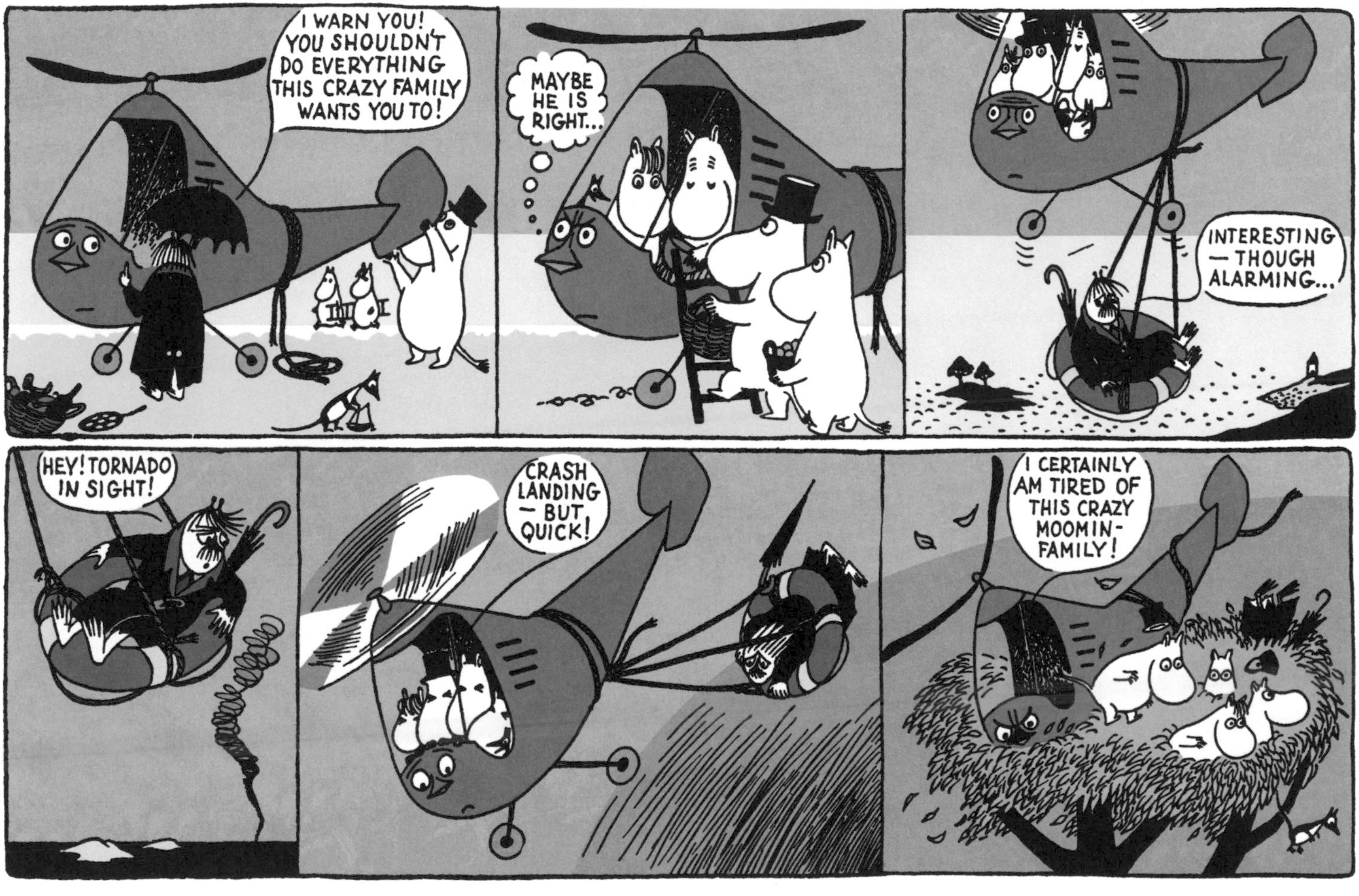
I WARN YOU! YOU SHOULDN'T DO EVERYTHING THIS CRAZY FAMILY WANTS YOU TO!
MAYBE HE IS RIGHT...
INTERESTING — THOUGH ALARMING...
HEY! TORNADO IN SIGHT!
CRASH LANDING — BUT QUICK!
I CERTAINLY AM TIRED OF THIS CRAZY MOOMIN-FAMILY!

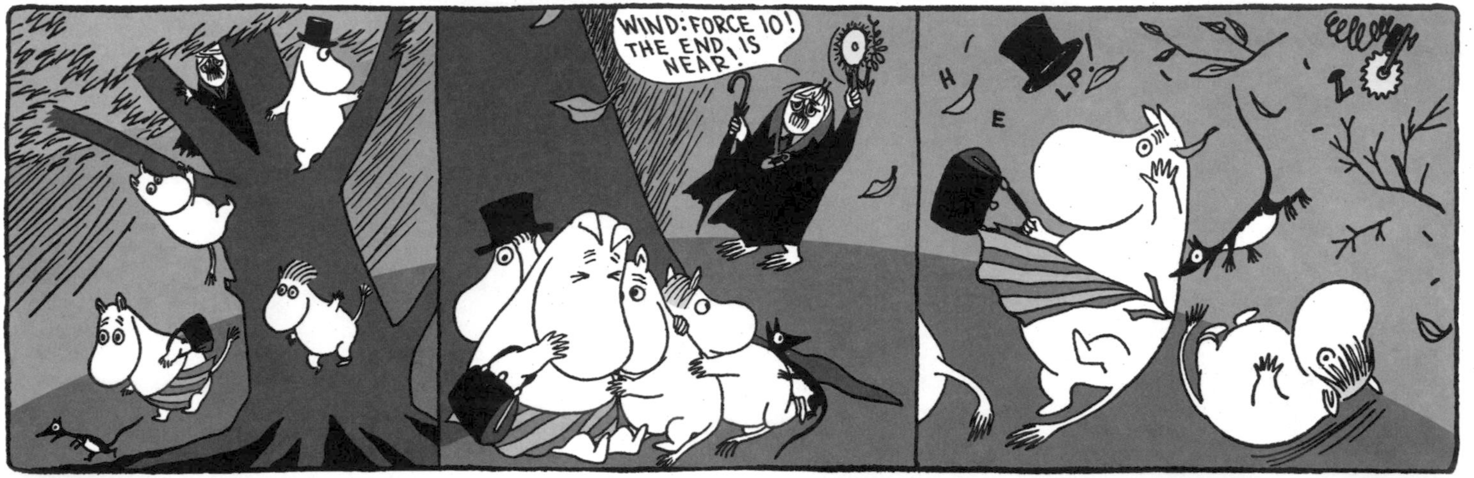
WIND: FORCE 10! THE END IS NEAR!
H E LP!

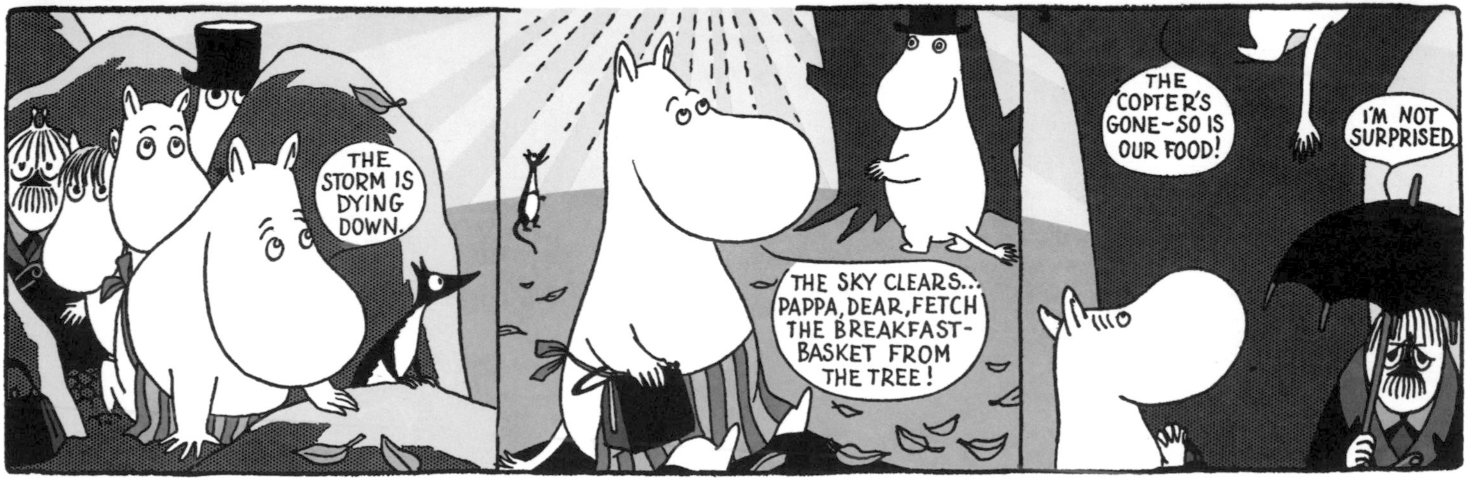
THE STORM IS DYING DOWN.
THE SKY CLEARS... PAPPA, DEAR, FETCH THE BREAKFAST-BASKET FROM THE TREE!
THE COPTER'S GONE-SO IS OUR FOOD!
I'M NOT SURPRISED.

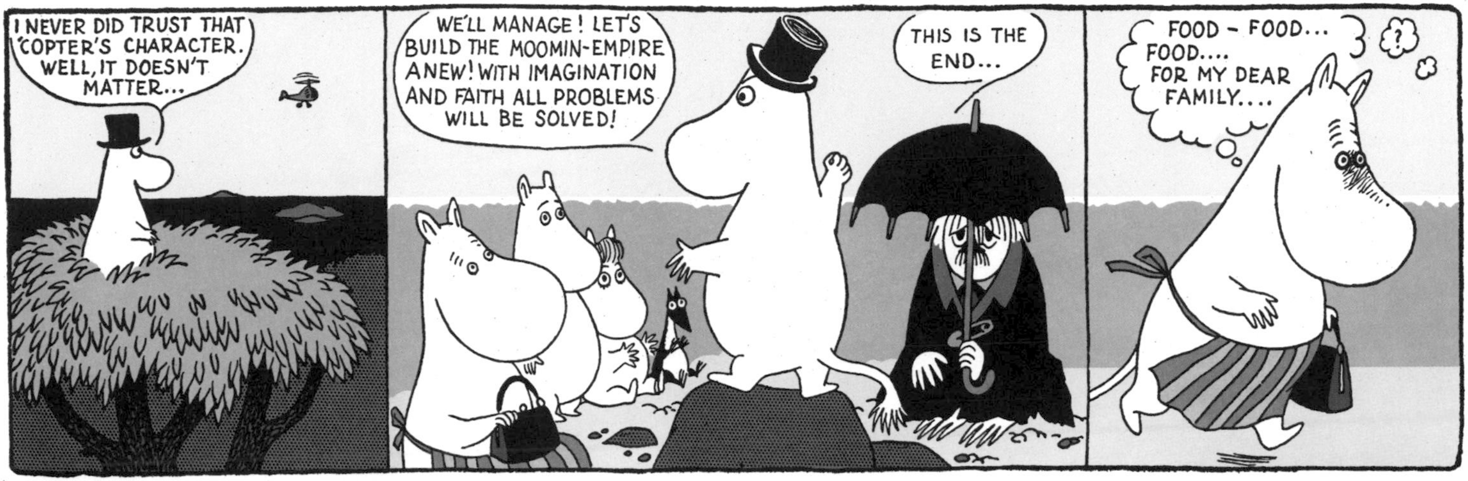
I NEVER DID TRUST THAT 'COPTER'S CHARACTER. WELL, IT DOESN'T MATTER...
WE'LL MANAGE! LET'S BUILD THE MOOMIN-EMPIRE ANEW! WITH IMAGINATION AND FAITH ALL PROBLEMS WILL BE SOLVED!
THIS IS THE END...
FOOD - FOOD... FOOD.... FOR MY DEAR FAMILY....
?

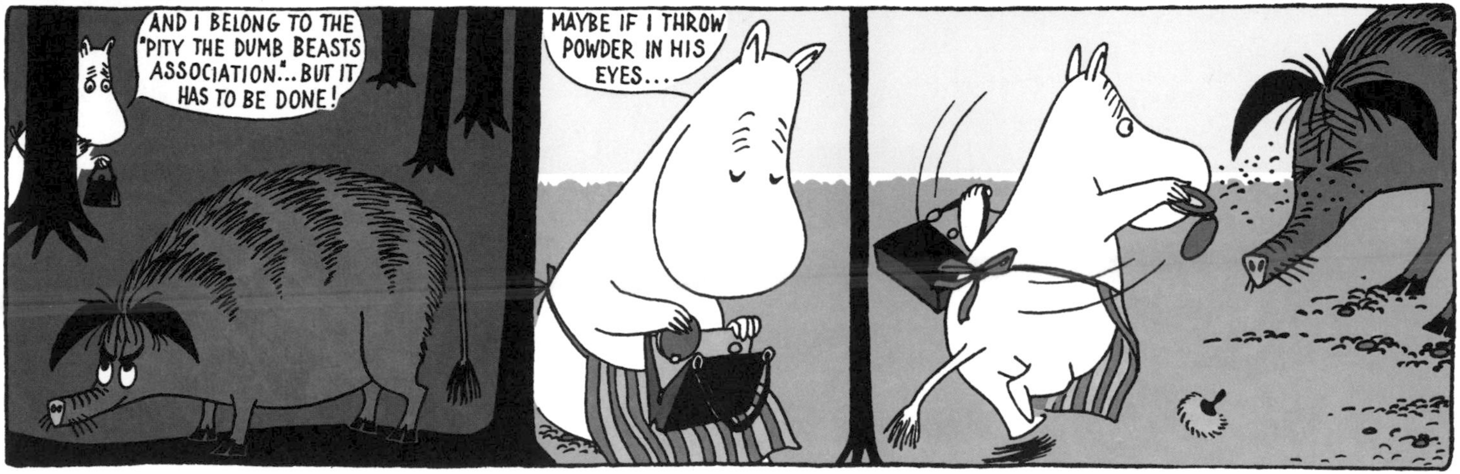
AND I BELONG TO THE "PITY THE DUMB BEASTS ASSOCIATION"... BUT IT HAS TO BE DONE!
MAYBE IF I THROW POWDER IN HIS EYES...

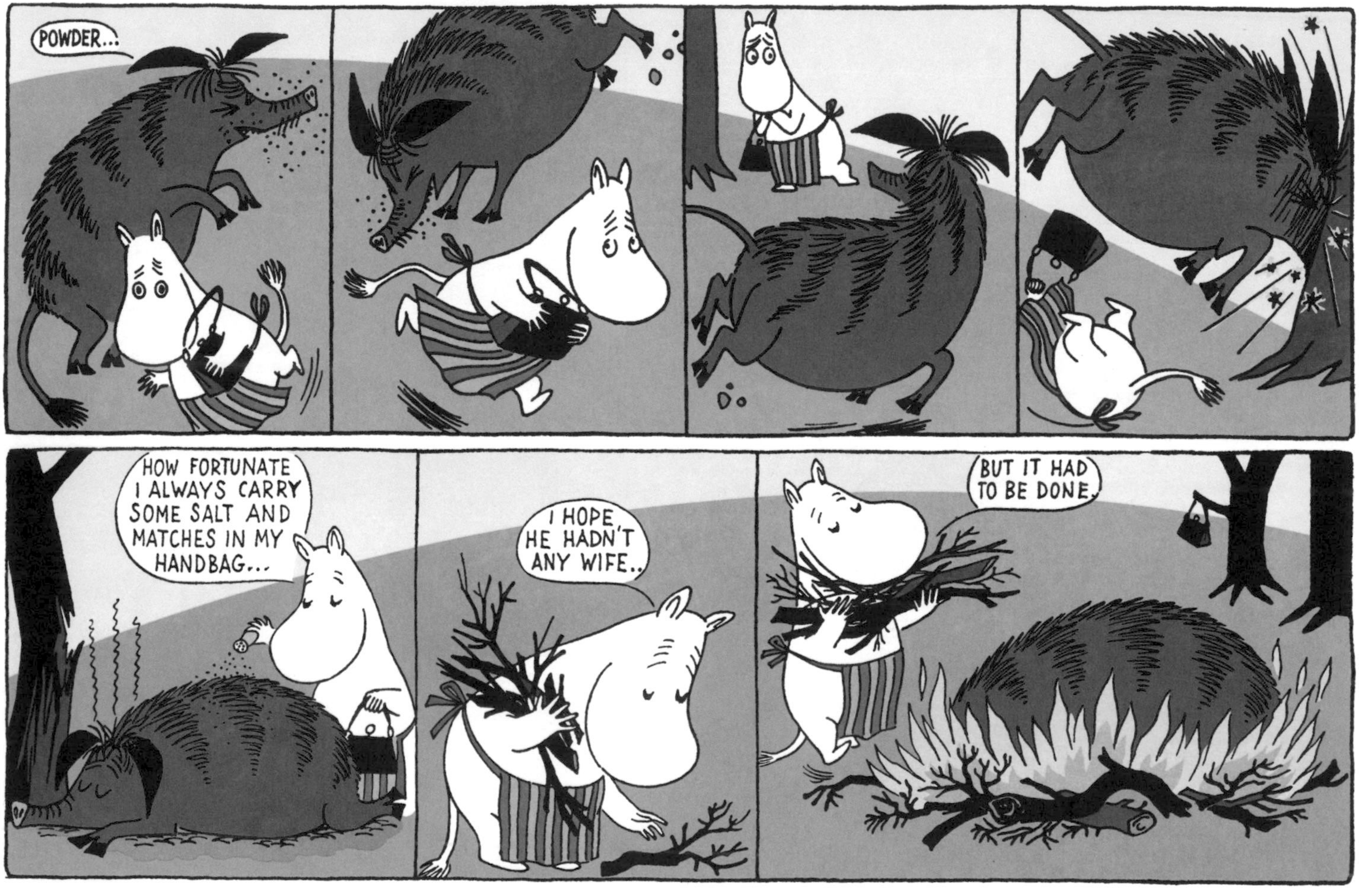
POWDER...
HOW FORTUNATE I ALWAYS CARRY SOME SALT AND MATCHES IN MY HANDBAG...
I HOPE HE HADN'T ANY WIFE..
BUT IT HAD TO BE DONE.

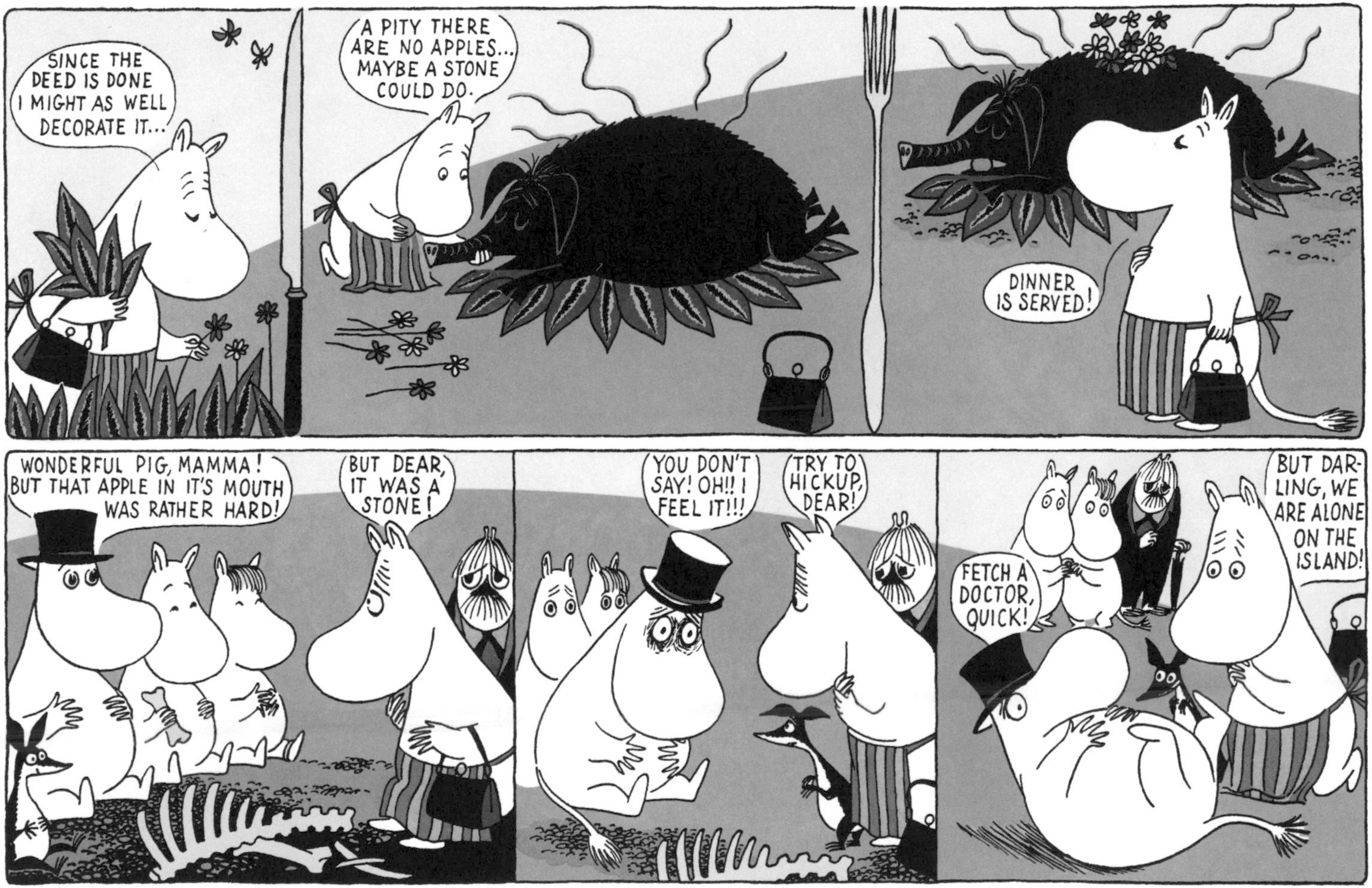
SINCE THE DEED IS DONE I MIGHT AS WELL DECORATE IT...
A PITY THERE ARE NO APPLES... MAYBE A STONE COULD DO.
DINNER IS SERVED!
WONDERFUL PIG, MAMMA! BUT THAT APPLE IN IT'S MOUTH WAS RATHER HARD!
BUT DEAR, IT WAS A STONE!
YOU DON'T SAY! OH!! I FEEL IT!!!
TRY TO HICKUP, DEAR!
FETCH A DOCTOR, QUICK!
BUT DAR-LING, WE ARE ALONE ON THE ISLAND!

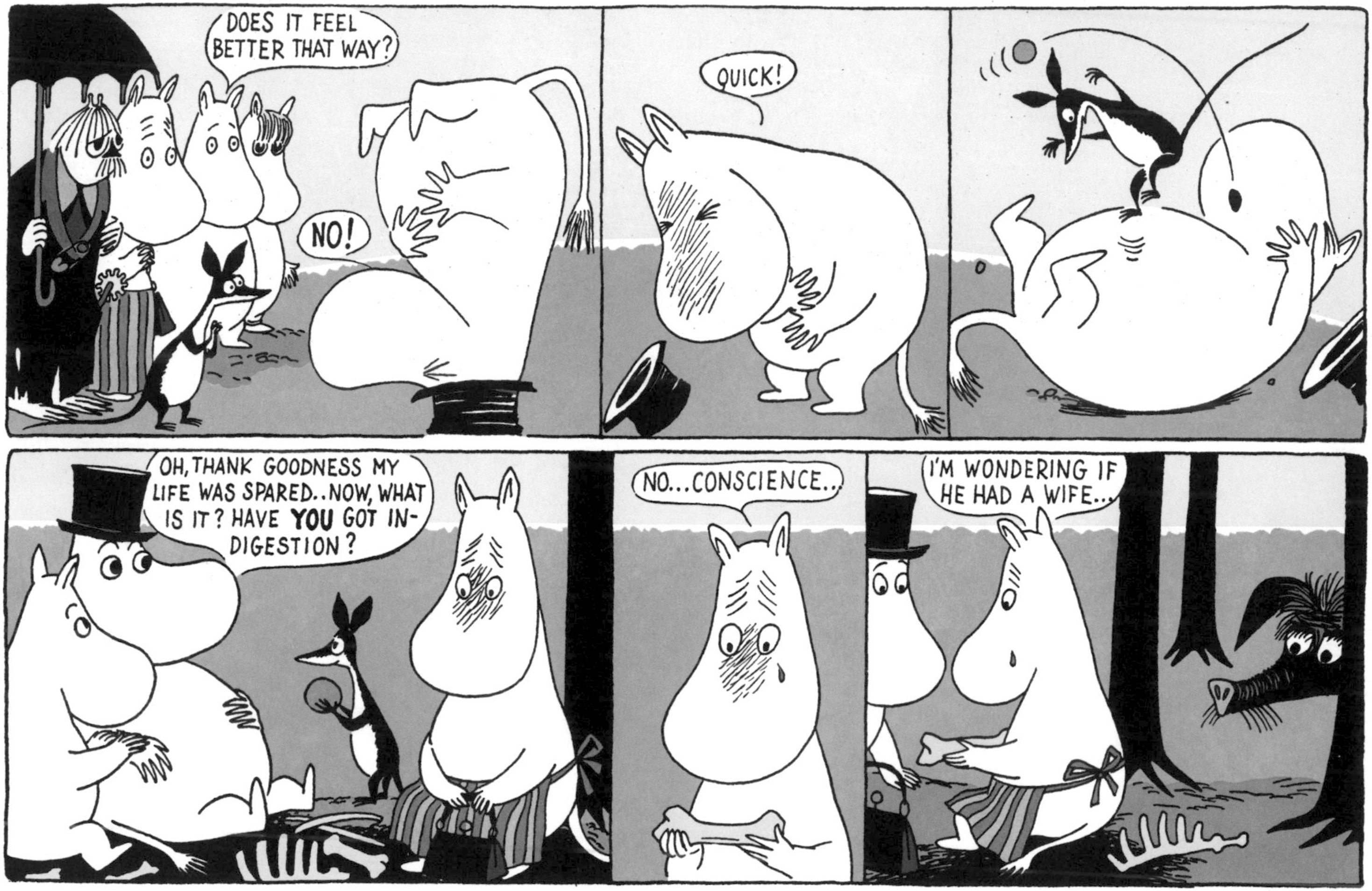
DOES IT FEEL BETTER THAT WAY?
NO!
QUICK!
OH, THANK GOODNESS MY LIFE WAS SPARED..NOW, WHAT IS IT? HAVE YOU GOT IN-DIGESTION?
NO...CONSCIENCE...
I'M WONDERING IF HE HAD A WIFE...

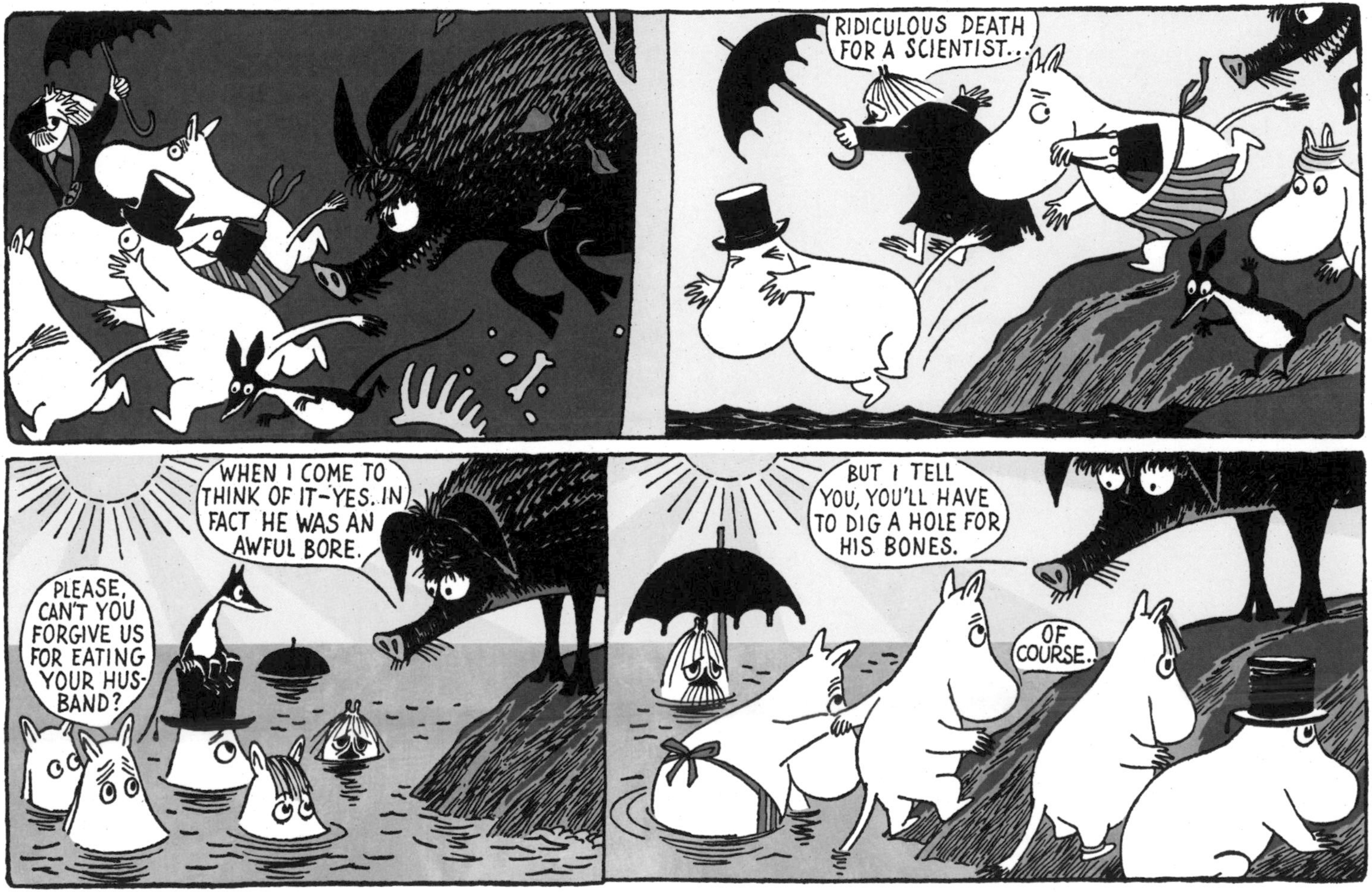
RIDICULOUS DEATH FOR A SCIENTIST...
PLEASE, CAN'T YOU FORGIVE US FOR EATING YOUR HUSBAND?
WHEN I COME TO THINK OF IT-YES. IN FACT HE WAS AN AWFUL BORE.
BUT I TELL YOU, YOU'LL HAVE TO DIG A HOLE FOR HIS BONES.
OF COURSE.

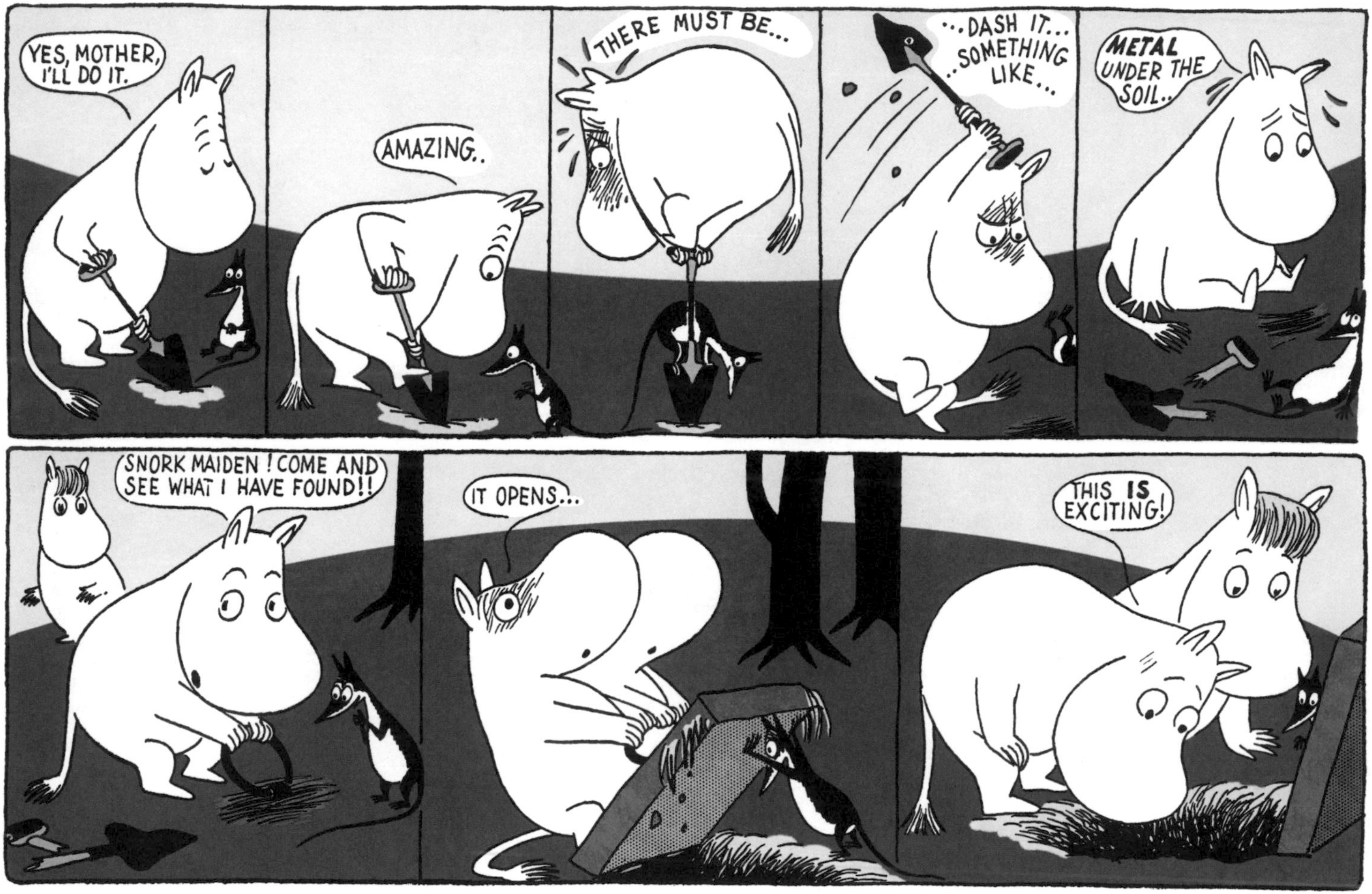
YES, MOTHER, I'LL DO IT.
AMAZING..
THERE MUST BE...
...DASH IT... ..SOMETHING LIKE...
METAL UNDER THE SOIL..
SNORK MAIDEN! COME AND SEE WHAT I HAVE FOUND!!
IT OPENS...
THIS IS EXCITING!

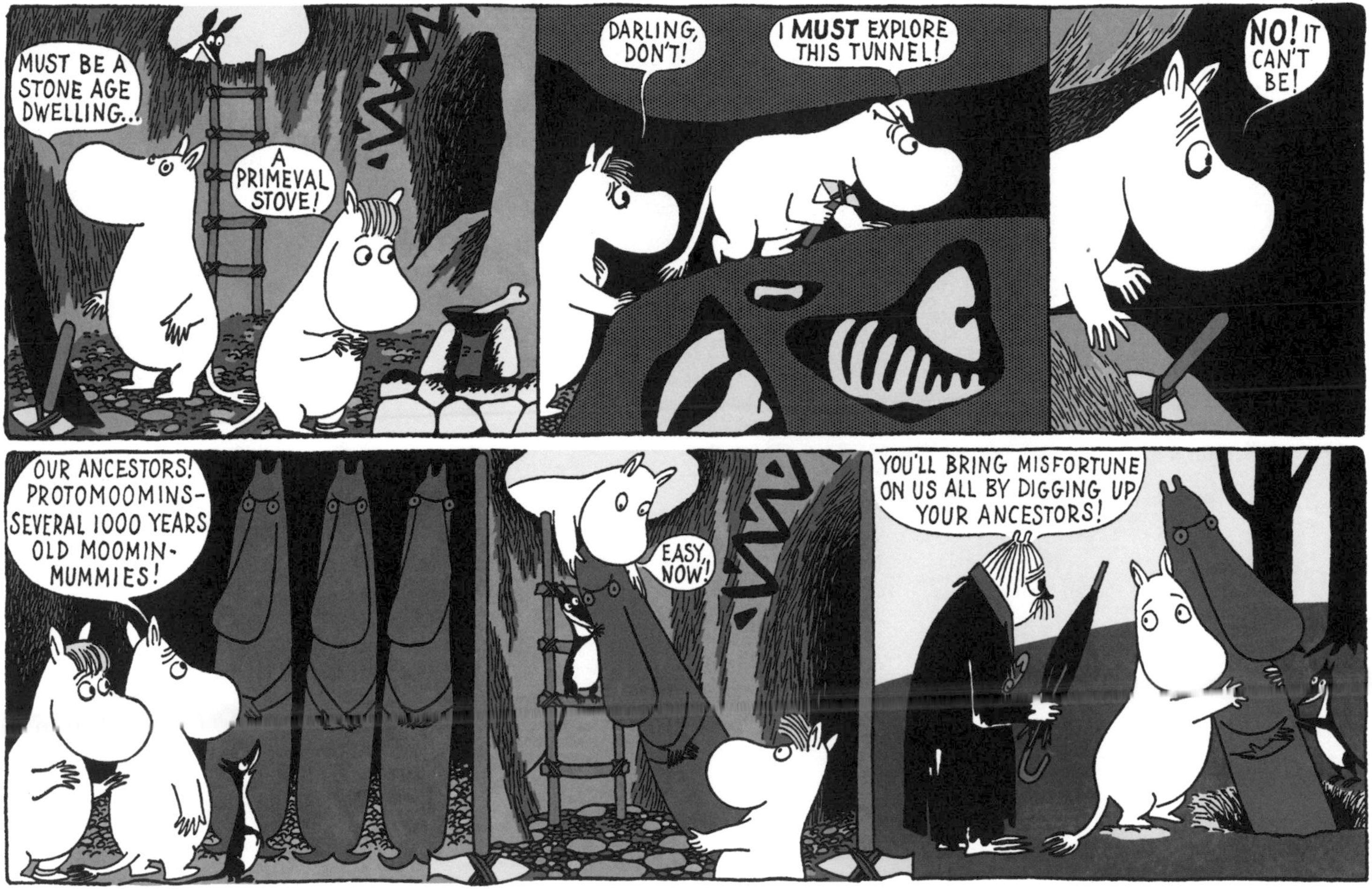
MUST BE A STONE AGE DWELLING...
A PRIMEVAL STOVE!
DARLING, DON'T!
I **MUST** EXPLORE THIS TUNNEL!
NO! IT CAN'T BE!
OUR ANCESTORS! PROTOMOOMINS-SEVERAL 1000 YEARS OLD MOOMIN-MUMMIES!
EASY, NOW!
YOU'LL BRING MISFORTUNE ON US ALL BY DIGGING UP YOUR ANCESTORS!

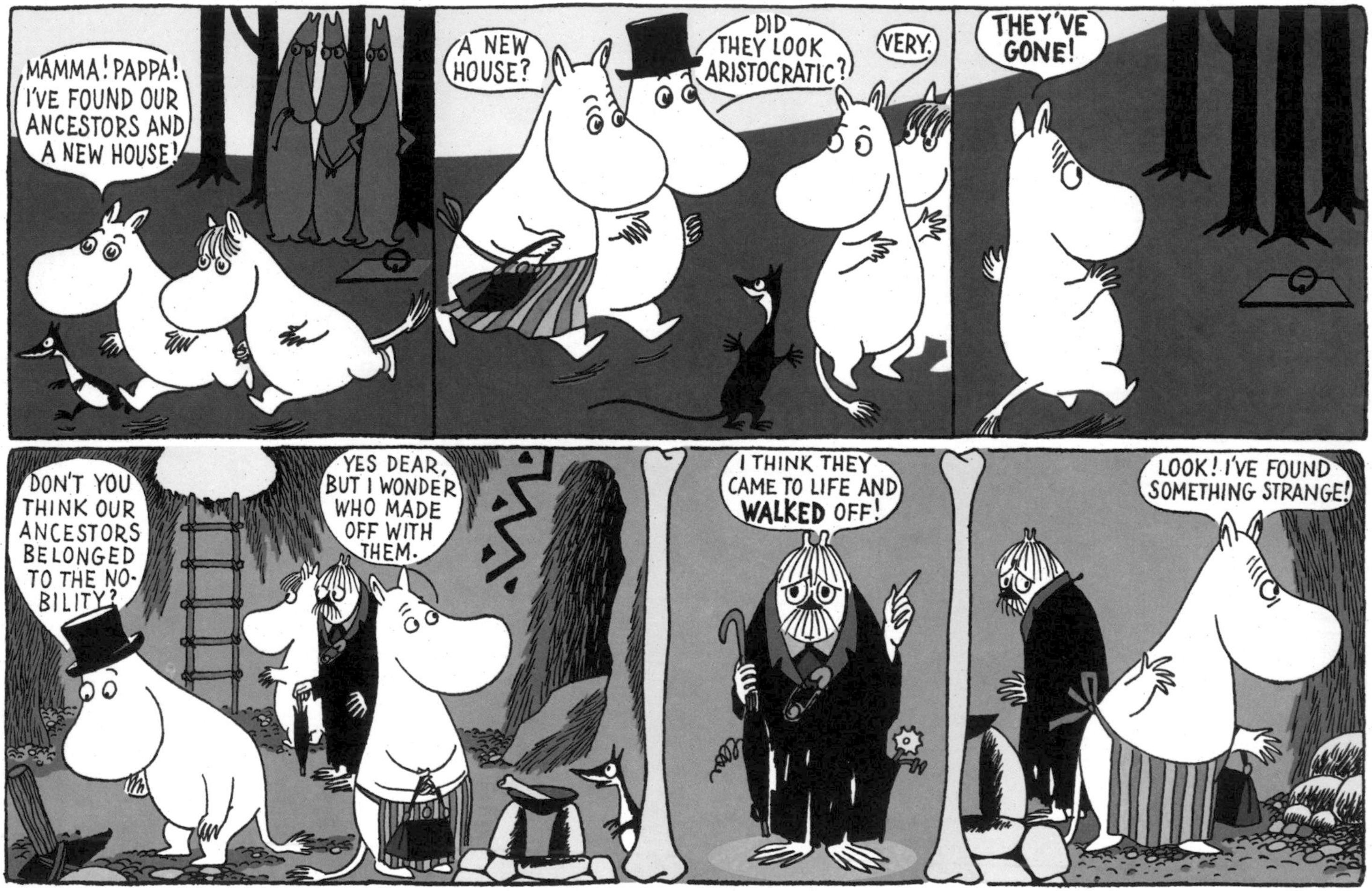
MAMMA! PAPPA! I'VE FOUND OUR ANCESTORS AND A NEW HOUSE!
A NEW HOUSE?
DID THEY LOOK ARISTOCRATIC?
VERY.
THEY'VE GONE!
DON'T YOU THINK OUR ANCESTORS BELONGED TO THE NO-BILITY?
YES DEAR, BUT I WONDER WHO MADE OFF WITH THEM.
I THINK THEY CAME TO LIFE AND **WALKED** OFF!
LOOK! I'VE FOUND SOMETHING STRANGE!

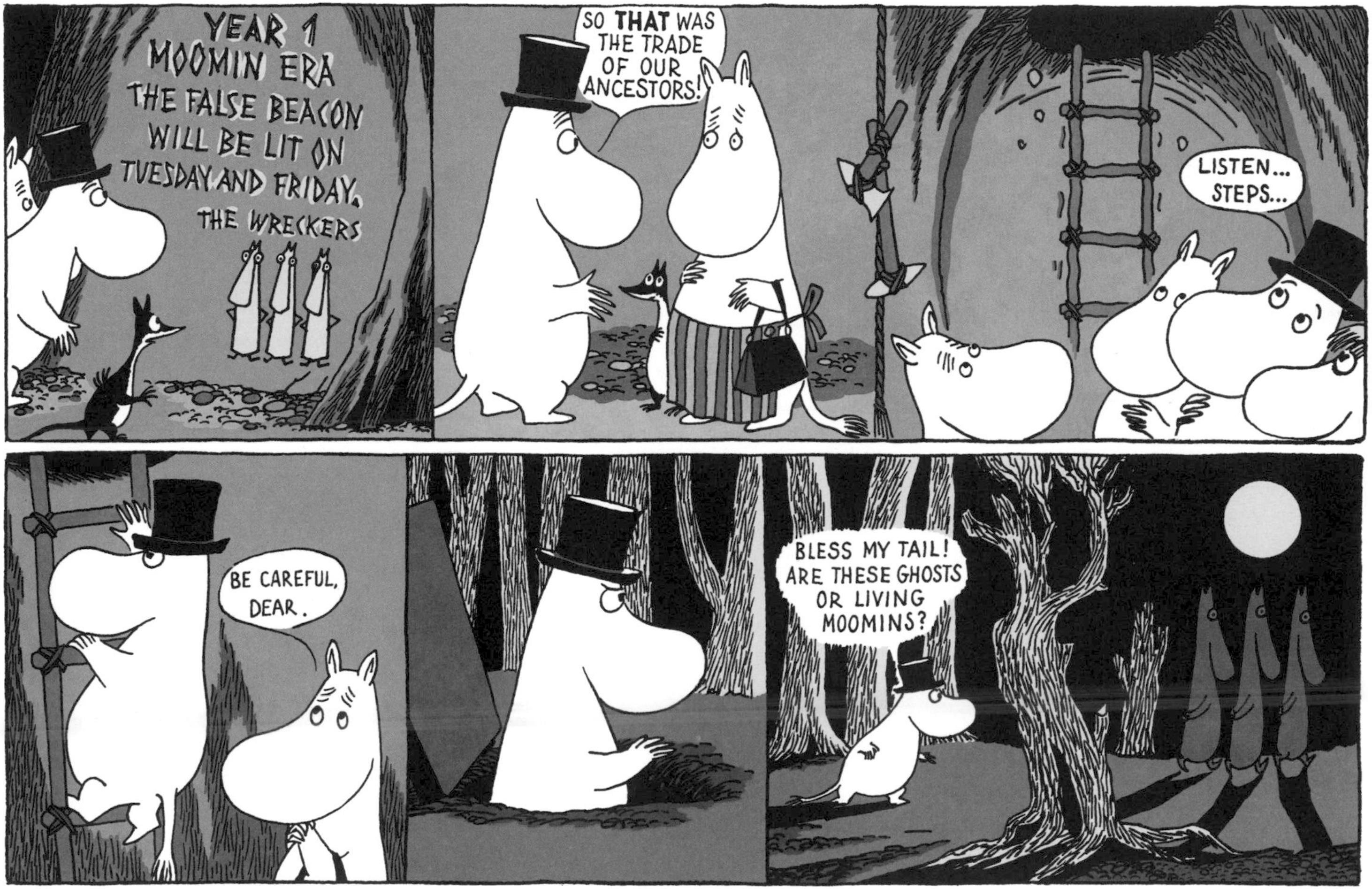
YEAR 1
MOOMIN ERA
THE FALSE BEACON
WILL BE LIT ON
TUESDAY AND FRIDAY.
THE WRECKERS
SO **THAT** WAS THE TRADE OF OUR ANCESTORS!
LISTEN... STEPS...
BE CAREFUL, DEAR.
BLESS MY TAIL! ARE THESE GHOSTS OR LIVING MOOMINS?

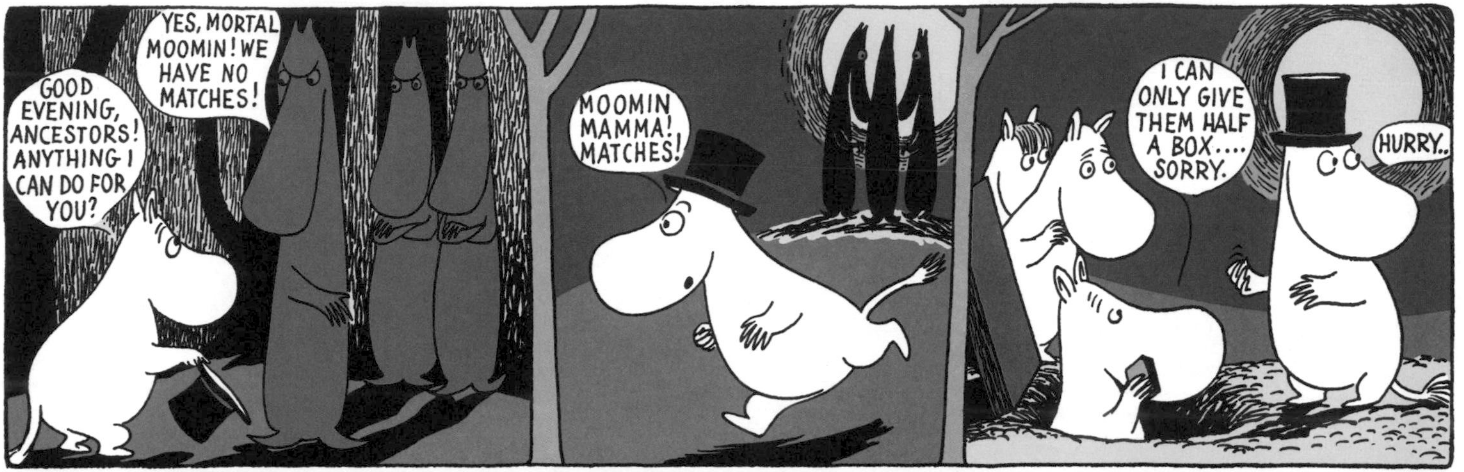
GOOD EVENING, ANCESTORS! ANYTHING I CAN DO FOR YOU?
YES, MORTAL MOOMIN! WE HAVE NO MATCHES!
MOOMIN MAMMA! MATCHES!
I CAN ONLY GIVE THEM HALF A BOX.... SORRY.
HURRY..

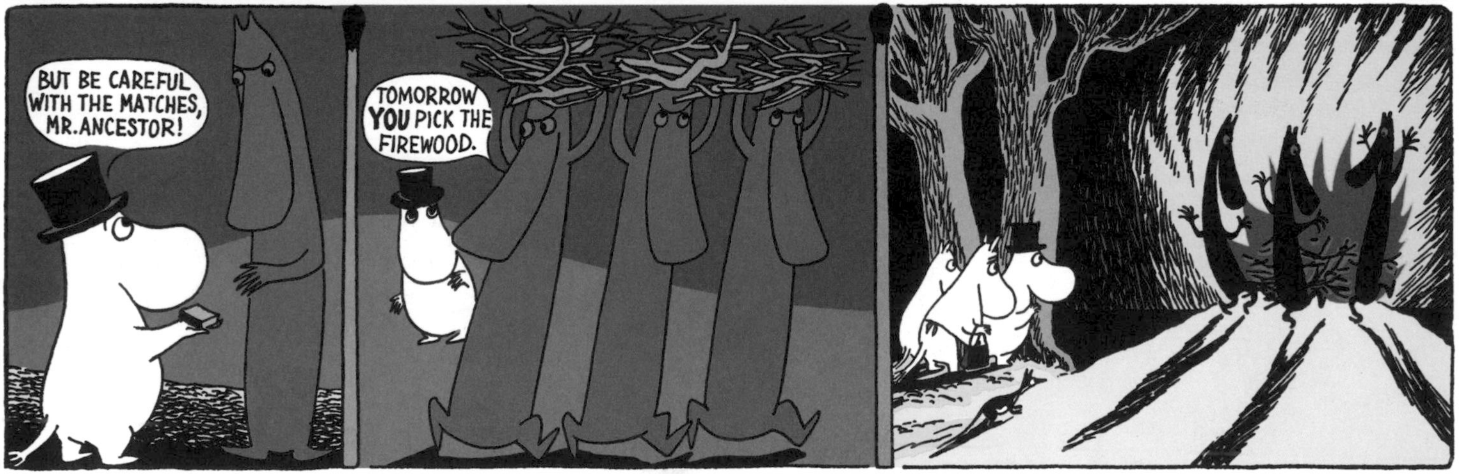
BUT BE CAREFUL WITH THE MATCHES, MR. ANCESTOR!
TOMORROW **YOU** PICK THE FIREWOOD.

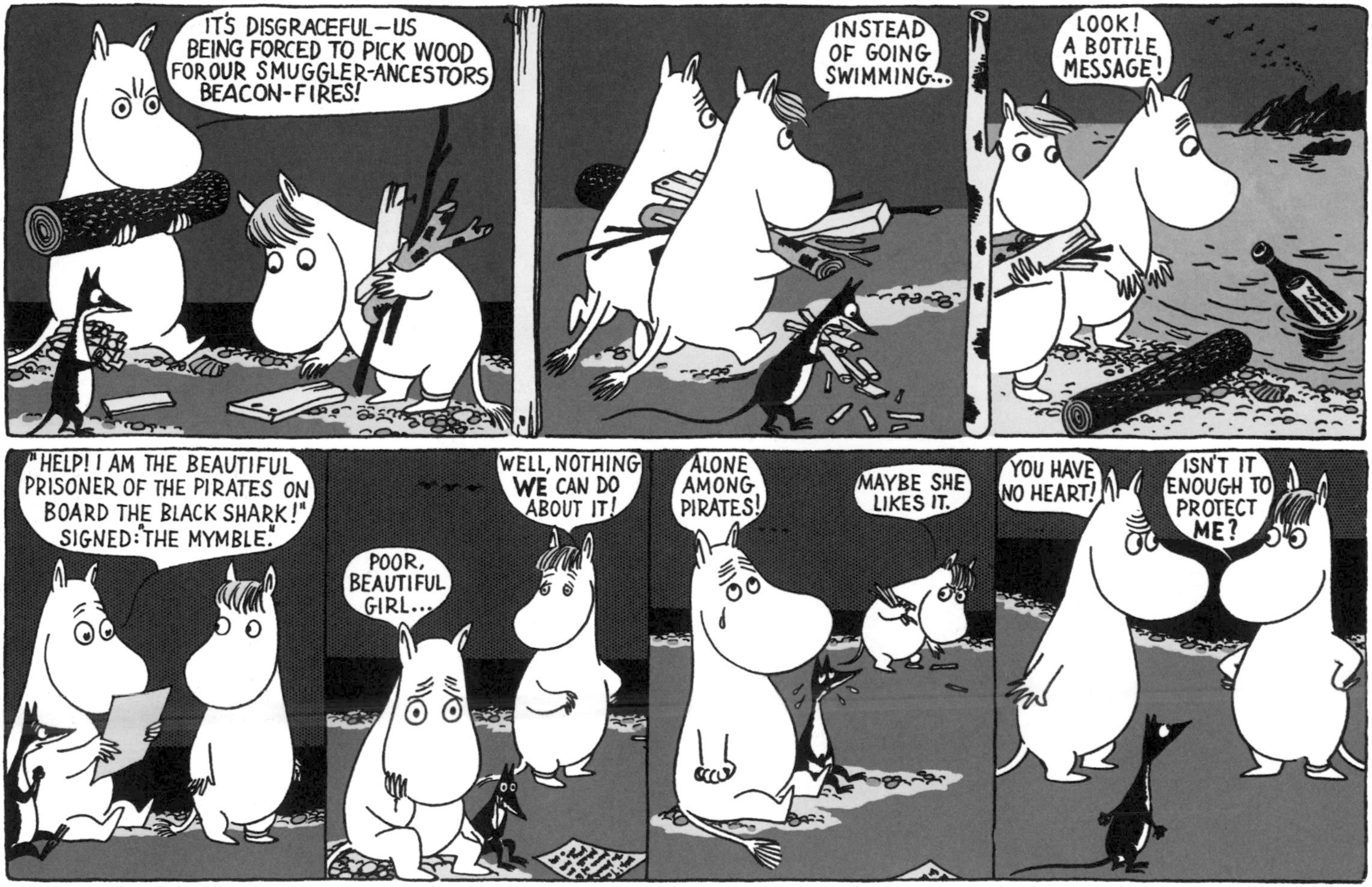
IT'S DISGRACEFUL—US BEING FORCED TO PICK WOOD FOR OUR SMUGGLER-ANCESTORS BEACON-FIRES!
INSTEAD OF GOING SWIMMING...
LOOK! A BOTTLE MESSAGE!
"HELP! I AM THE BEAUTIFUL PRISONER OF THE PIRATES ON BOARD THE BLACK SHARK!" SIGNED: "THE MYMBLE."
POOR, BEAUTIFUL GIRL...
WELL, NOTHING WE CAN DO ABOUT IT!
ALONE AMONG PIRATES!
MAYBE SHE LIKES IT.
YOU HAVE NO HEART!
ISN'T IT ENOUGH TO PROTECT ME?

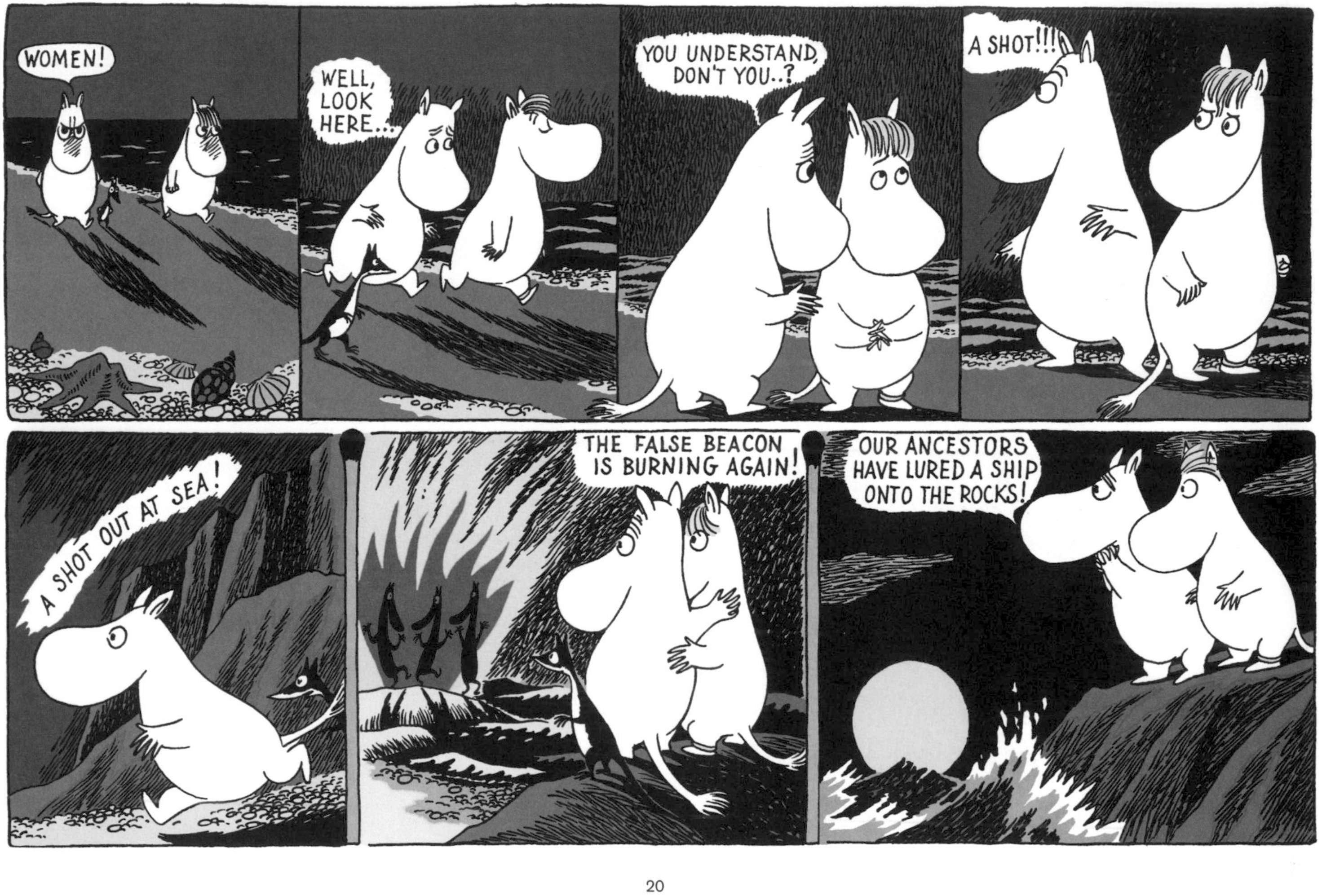

WOMEN!
WELL, LOOK HERE...
YOU UNDERSTAND, DON'T YOU..?
A SHOT!!!
A SHOT OUT AT SEA!
THE FALSE BEACON IS BURNING AGAIN!
OUR ANCESTORS HAVE LURED A SHIP ONTO THE ROCKS!

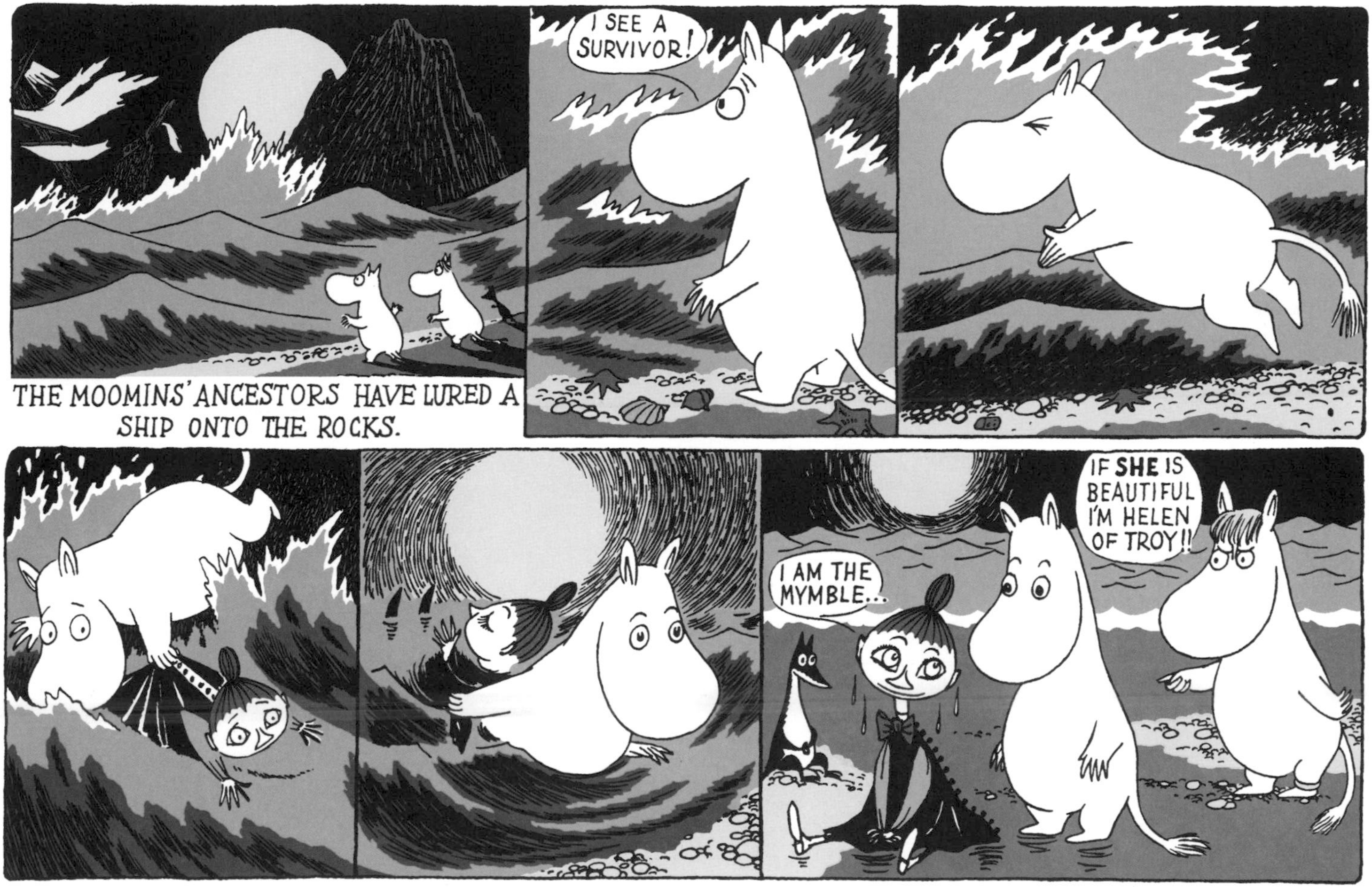
THE MOOMINS' ANCESTORS HAVE LURED A SHIP ONTO THE ROCKS.
I SEE A SURVIVOR!
I AM THE MYMBLE...
IF **SHE** IS BEAUTIFUL I'M HELEN OF TROY!!

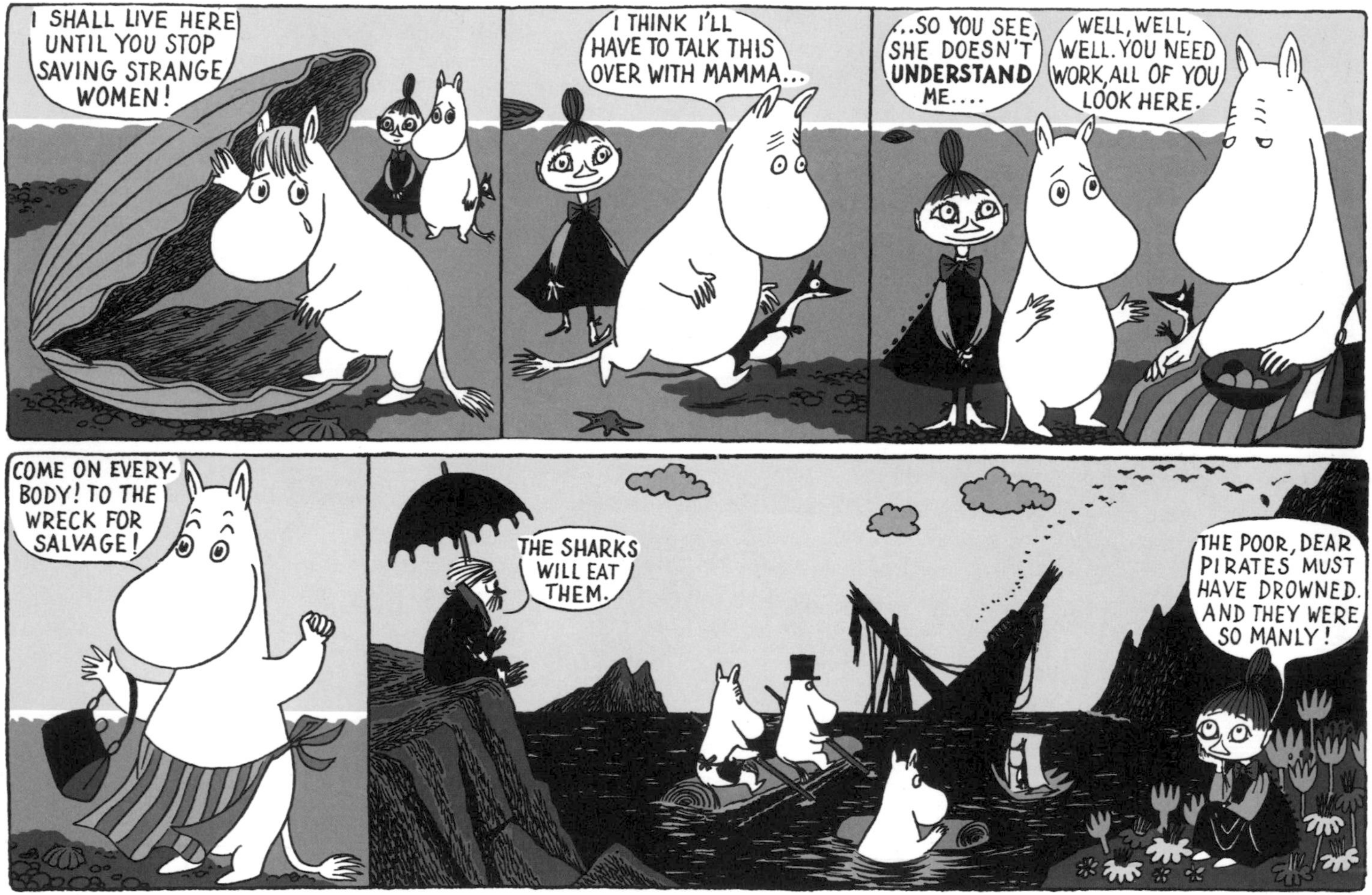
I SHALL LIVE HERE UNTIL YOU STOP SAVING STRANGE WOMEN!
I THINK I'LL HAVE TO TALK THIS OVER WITH MAMMA...
...SO YOU SEE, SHE DOESN'T **UNDERSTAND** ME....
WELL, WELL, WELL. YOU NEED WORK, ALL OF YOU LOOK HERE.
COME ON EVERY-BODY! TO THE WRECK FOR SALVAGE!
THE SHARKS WILL EAT THEM.
THE POOR, DEAR PIRATES MUST HAVE DROWNED. AND THEY WERE SO MANLY!

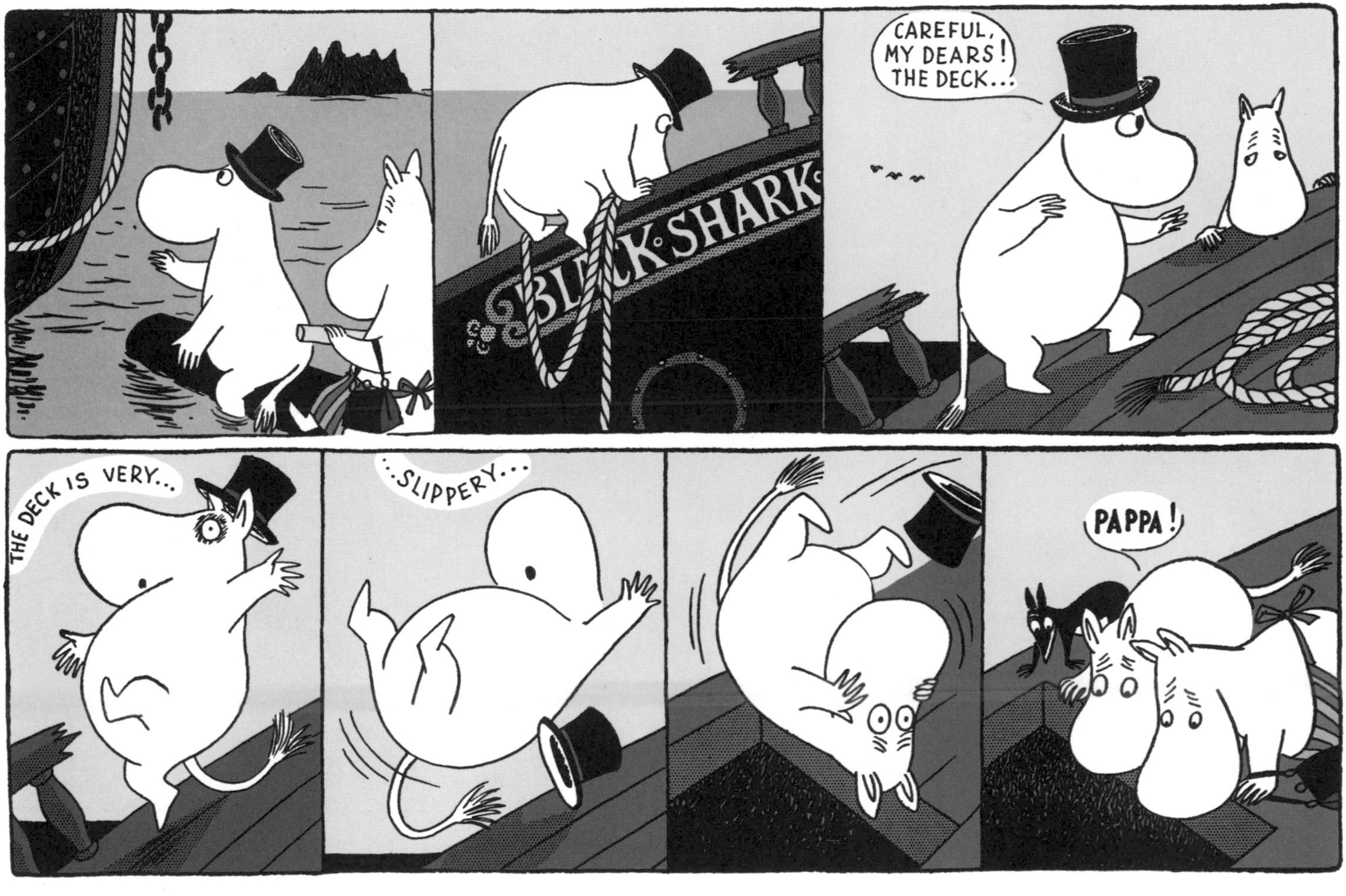
SHARK
CAREFUL, MY DEARS! THE DECK...
THE DECK IS VERY...
...SLIPPERY...
PAPPA!

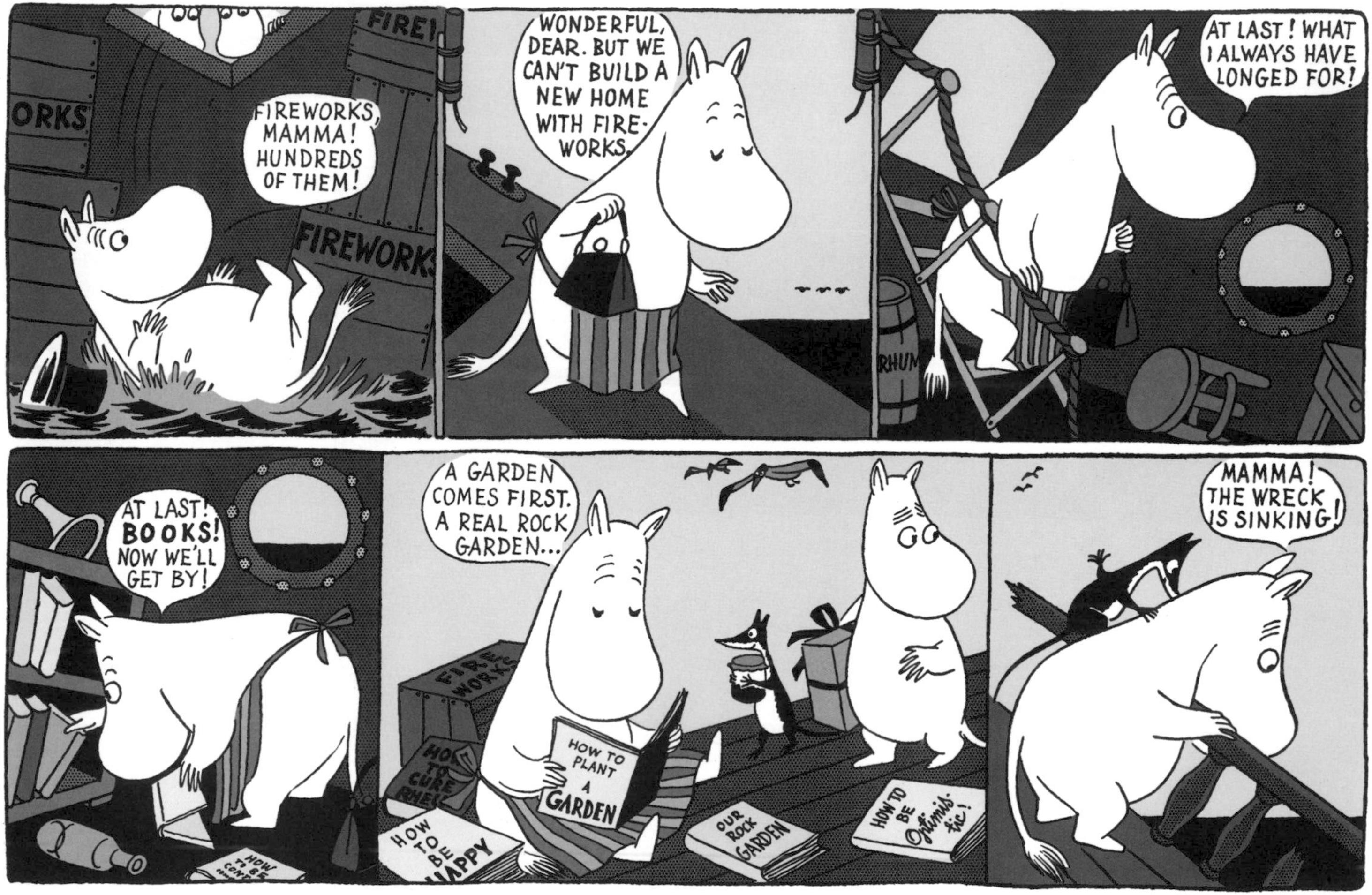

FIREWORKS, MAMMA! HUNDREDS OF THEM!
FIREWORKS
WONDERFUL, DEAR. BUT WE CAN'T BUILD A NEW HOME WITH FIRE-WORKS.
AT LAST! WHAT I ALWAYS HAVE LONGED FOR!
RHUM
AT LAST! BOOKS! NOW WE'LL GET BY!
A GARDEN COMES FIRST. A REAL ROCK GARDEN...
HOW TO PLANT A GARDEN
OUR ROCK GARDEN
MAMMA! THE WRECK IS SINKING!

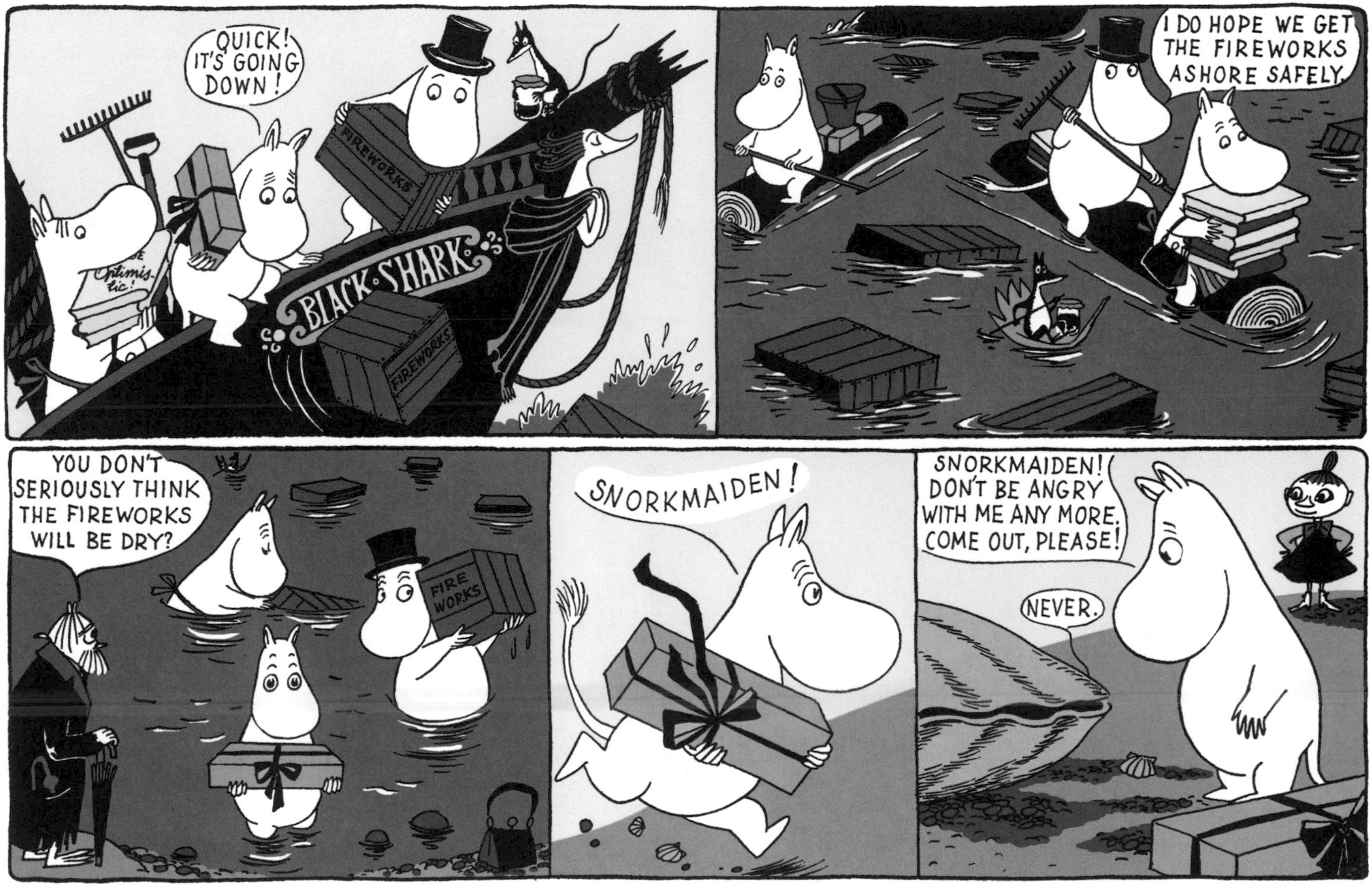
QUICK! IT'S GOING DOWN!
FIREWORKS
BLACK SHARK
FIREWORKS
I DO HOPE WE GET THE FIREWORKS ASHORE SAFELY.
YOU DON'T SERIOUSLY THINK THE FIREWORKS WILL BE DRY?
FIRE WORKS
SNORKMAIDEN!
SNORKMAIDEN! DON'T BE ANGRY WITH ME ANY MORE, COME OUT, PLEASE!
NEVER.

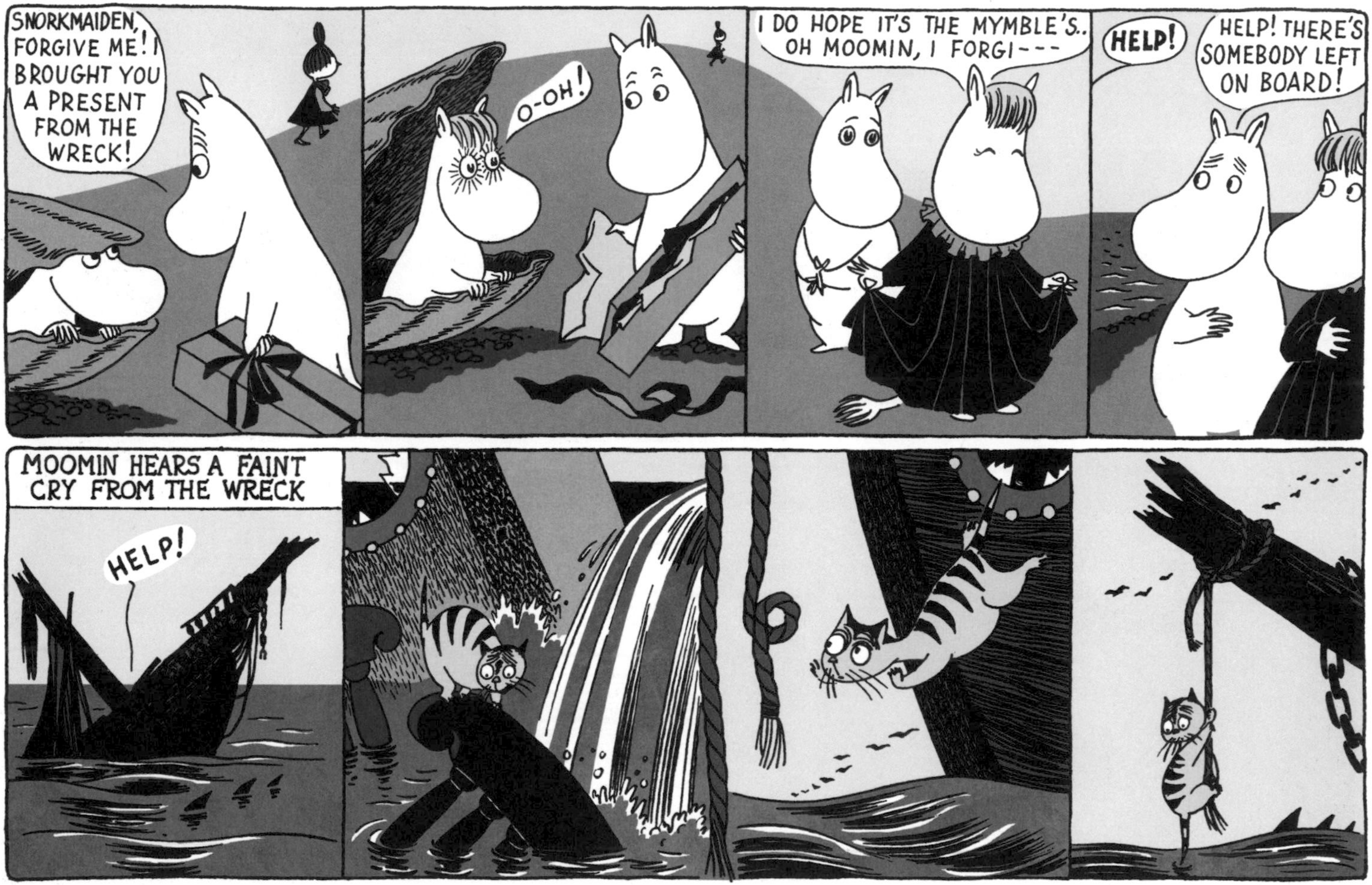
SNORKMAIDEN, FORGIVE ME! I BROUGHT YOU A PRESENT FROM THE WRECK!
O-OH!
I DO HOPE IT'S THE MYMBLE'S.. OH MOOMIN, I FORGI---
HELP!
HELP! THERE'S SOMEBODY LEFT ON BOARD!
MOOMIN HEARS A FAINT CRY FROM THE WRECK
HELP!

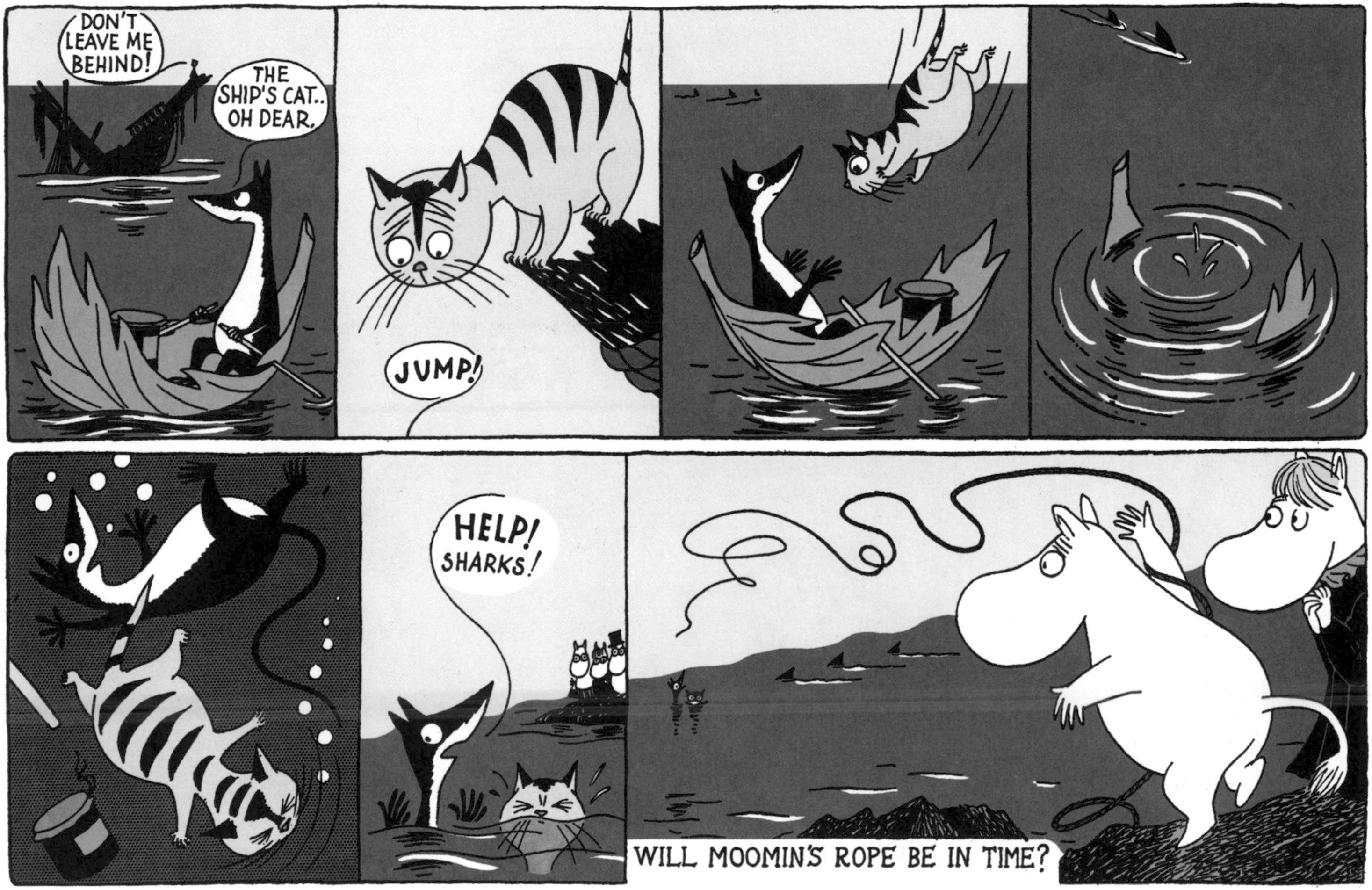
DON'T LEAVE ME BEHIND!
THE SHIP'S CAT.. OH DEAR.
JUMP!
HELP! SHARKS!
WILL MOOMIN'S ROPE BE IN TIME?

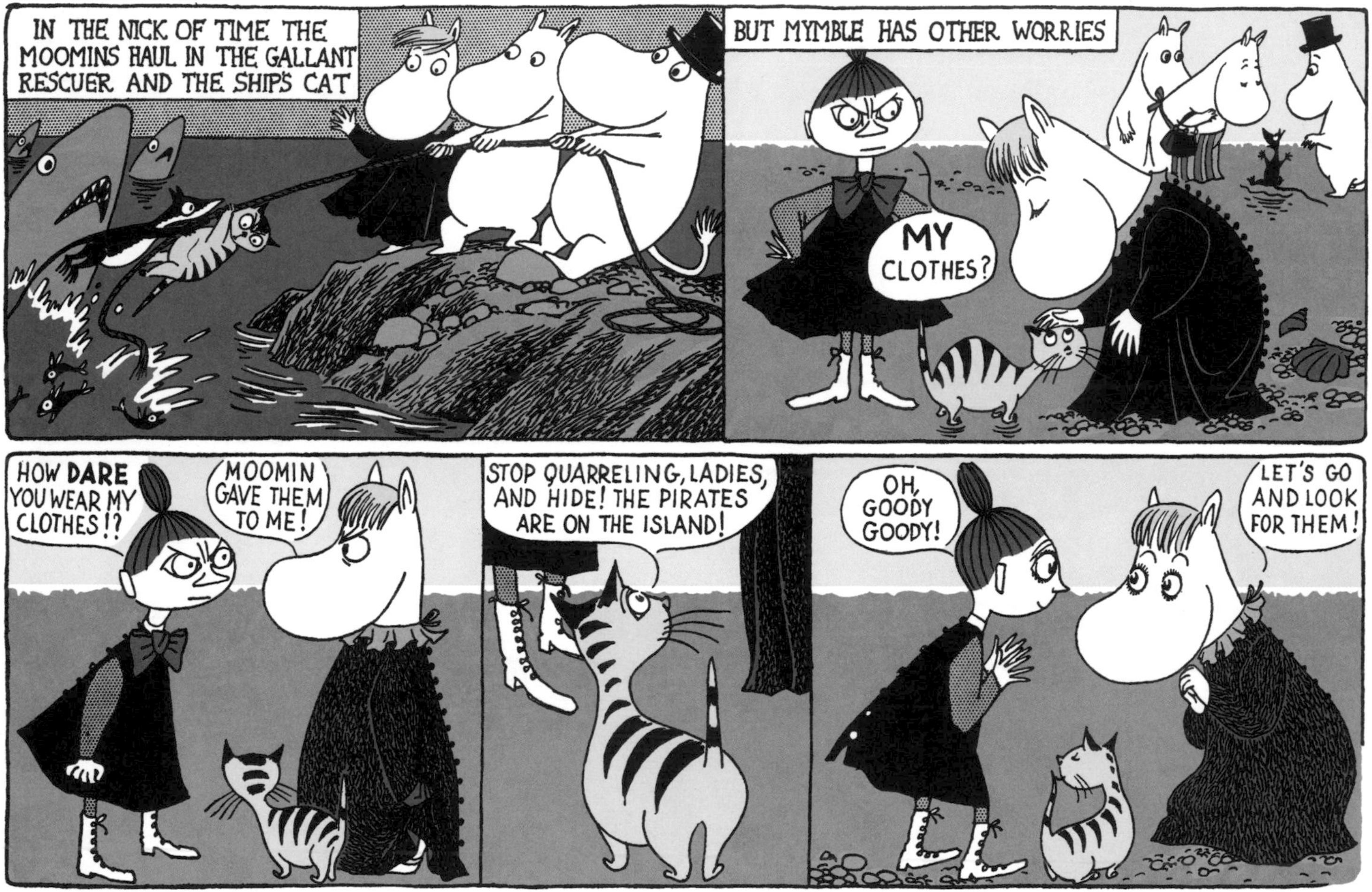
IN THE NICK OF TIME THE MOOMINS HAUL IN THE GALLANT RESCUER AND THE SHIP'S CAT
BUT MYMBLE HAS OTHER WORRIES
MY CLOTHES?
HOW DARE YOU WEAR MY CLOTHES!?
MOOMIN GAVE THEM TO ME!
STOP QUARRELING, LADIES, AND HIDE! THE PIRATES ARE ON THE ISLAND!
OH, GOODY GOODY!
LET'S GO AND LOOK FOR THEM!

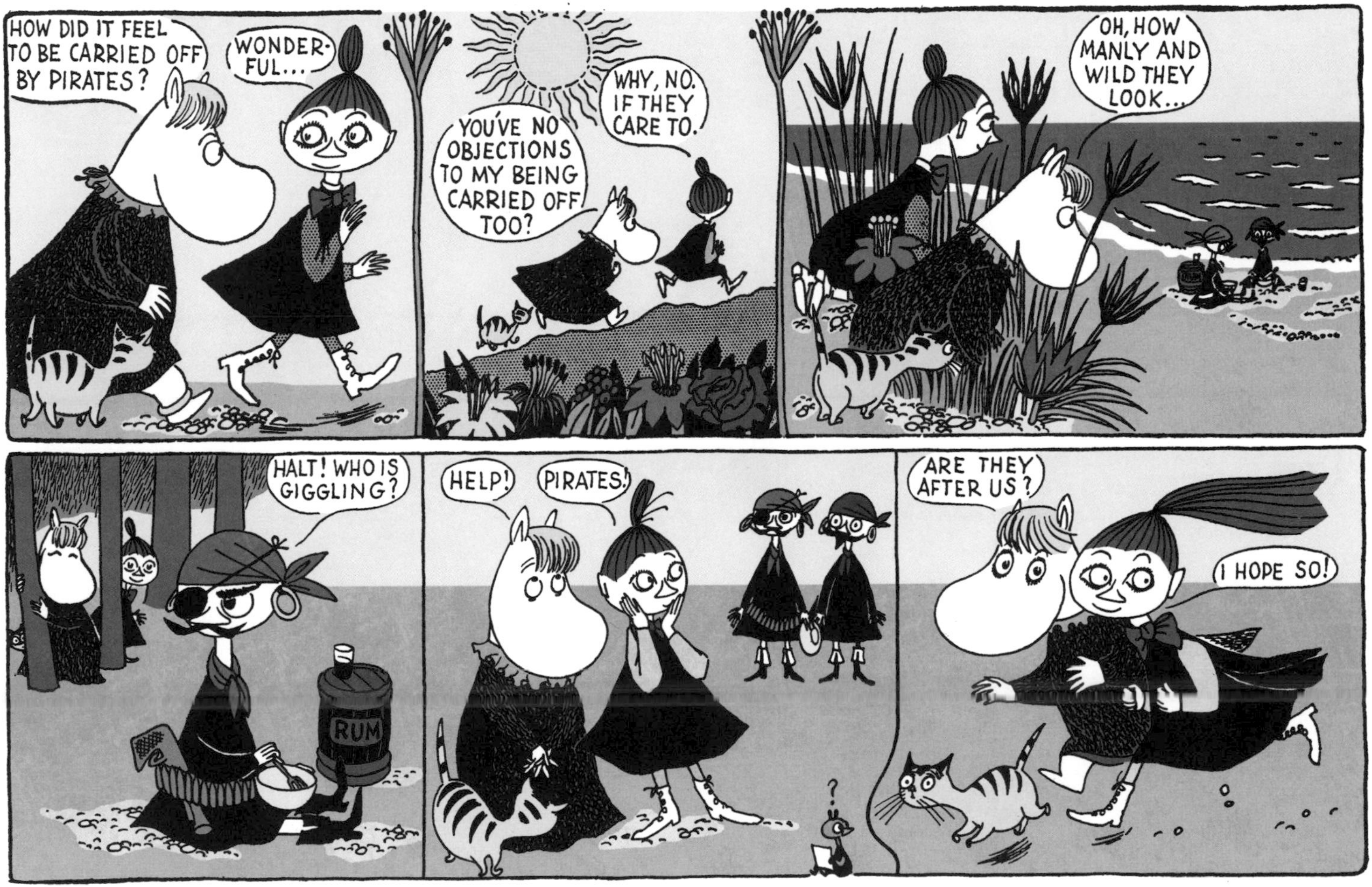
HOW DID IT FEEL TO BE CARRIED OFF BY PIRATES?
WONDER-FUL...
YOU'VE NO OBJECTIONS TO MY BEING CARRIED OFF TOO?
WHY, NO. IF THEY CARE TO.
OH, HOW MANLY AND WILD THEY LOOK...
HALT! WHO IS GIGGLING?
RUM
HELP!
PIRATES!
?
ARE THEY AFTER US?
I HOPE SO!

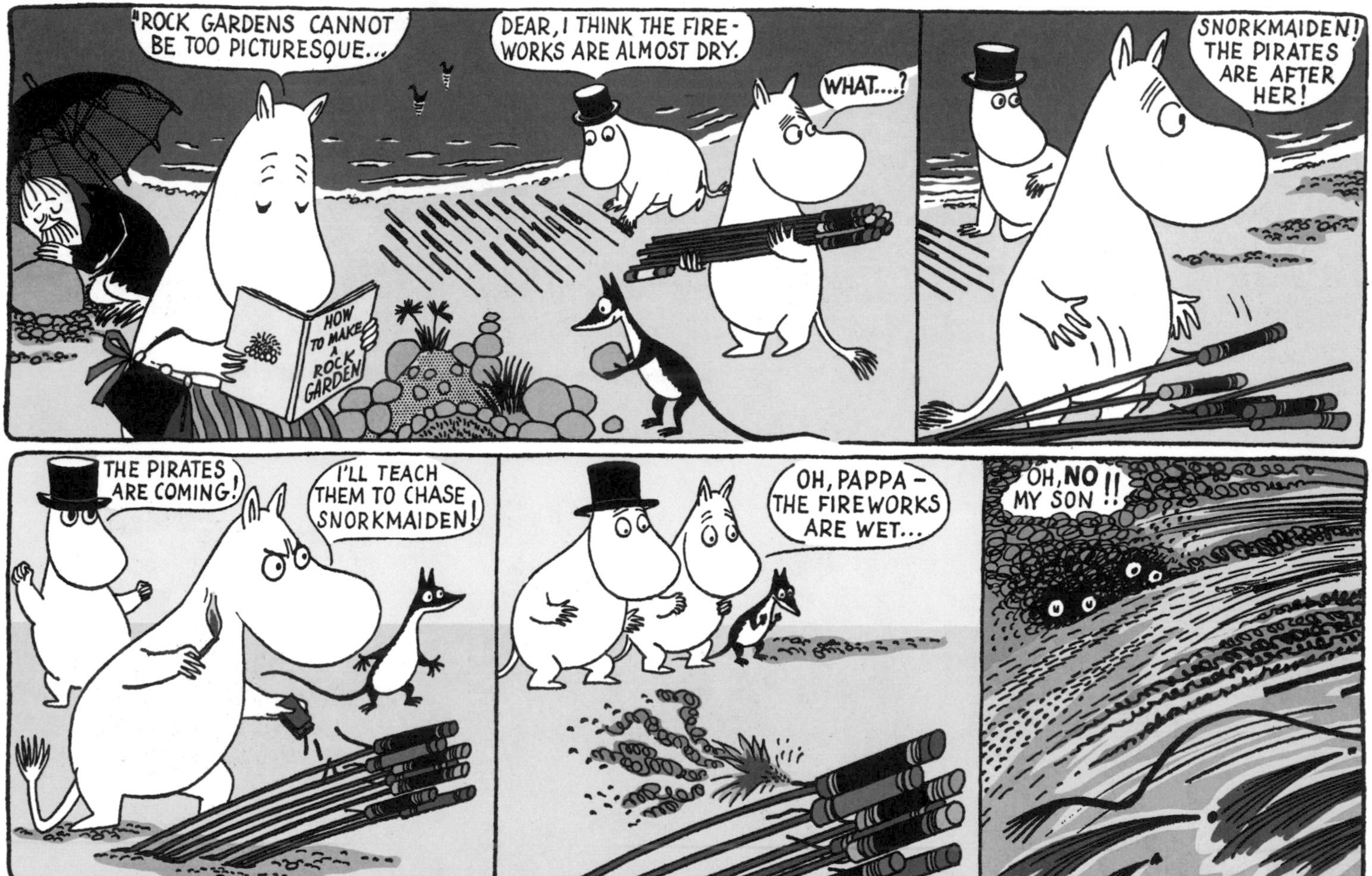
"ROCK GARDENS CANNOT BE TOO PICTURESQUE...
HOW TO MAKE A ROCK GARDEN
DEAR, I THINK THE FIRE-WORKS ARE ALMOST DRY.
WHAT....?
SNORKMAIDEN! THE PIRATES ARE AFTER HER!
THE PIRATES ARE COMING!
I'LL TEACH THEM TO CHASE SNORKMAIDEN!
OH, PAPPA - THE FIREWORKS ARE WET...
OH, NO MY SON!!

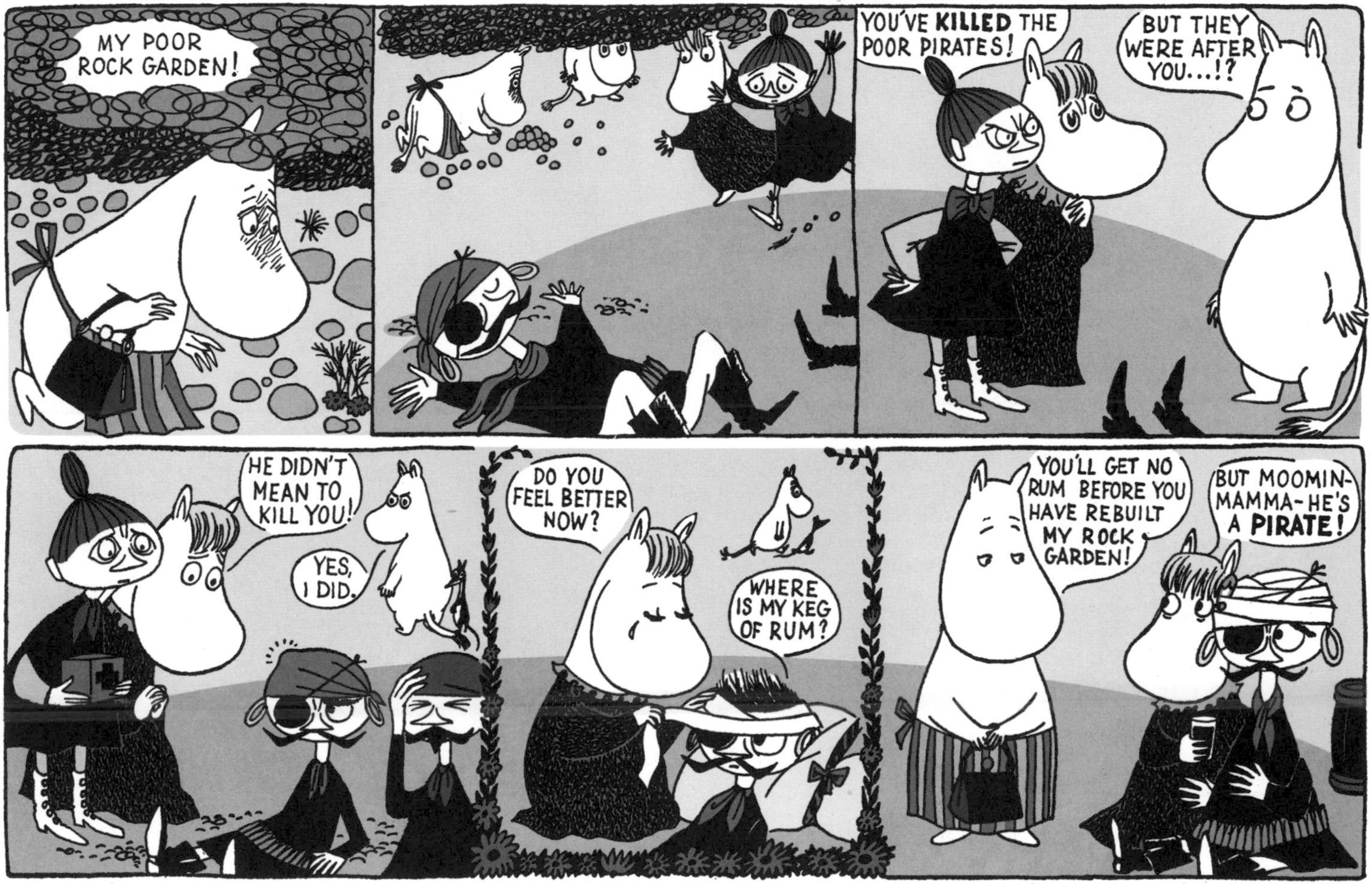

MY POOR ROCK GARDEN!
YOU'VE KILLED THE POOR PIRATES!
BUT THEY WERE AFTER YOU...!?
HE DIDN'T MEAN TO KILL YOU!
YES, I DID.
DO YOU FEEL BETTER NOW?
WHERE IS MY KEG OF RUM?
YOU'LL GET NO RUM BEFORE YOU HAVE REBUILT MY ROCK GARDEN!
BUT MOOMIN-MAMMA-HE'S A PIRATE!

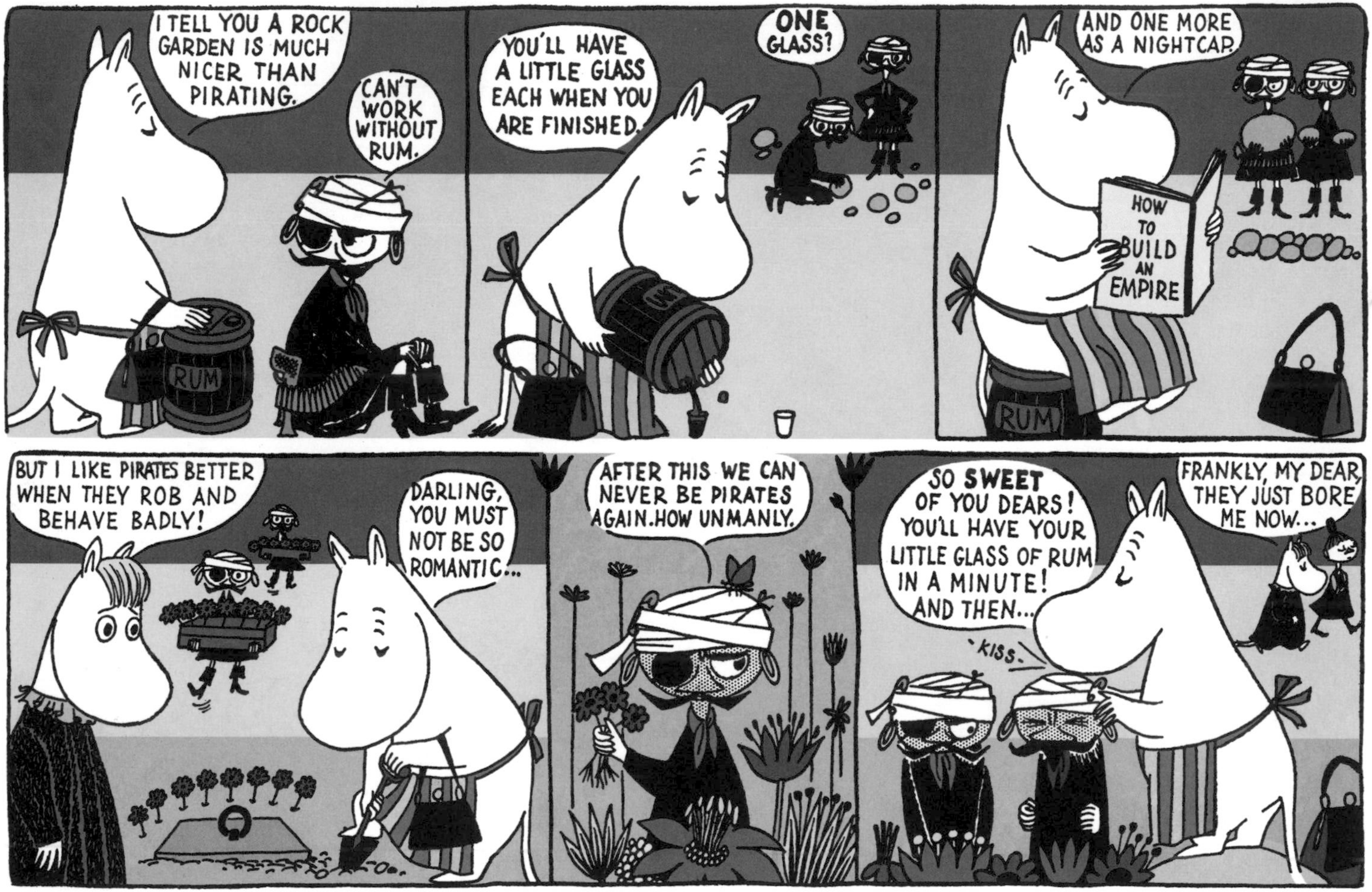
I TELL YOU A ROCK GARDEN IS MUCH NICER THAN PIRATING.
CAN'T WORK WITHOUT RUM.
RUM
YOU'LL HAVE A LITTLE GLASS EACH WHEN YOU ARE FINISHED.
ONE GLASS?
AND ONE MORE AS A NIGHTCAP.
HOW TO BUILD AN EMPIRE
RUM
BUT I LIKE PIRATES BETTER WHEN THEY ROB AND BEHAVE BADLY!
DARLING, YOU MUST NOT BE SO ROMANTIC...
AFTER THIS WE CAN NEVER BE PIRATES AGAIN. HOW UNMANLY.
SO **SWEET** OF YOU DEARS! YOU'LL HAVE YOUR LITTLE GLASS OF RUM IN A MINUTE! AND THEN...
FRANKLY, MY DEAR, THEY JUST BORE ME NOW...
KISS

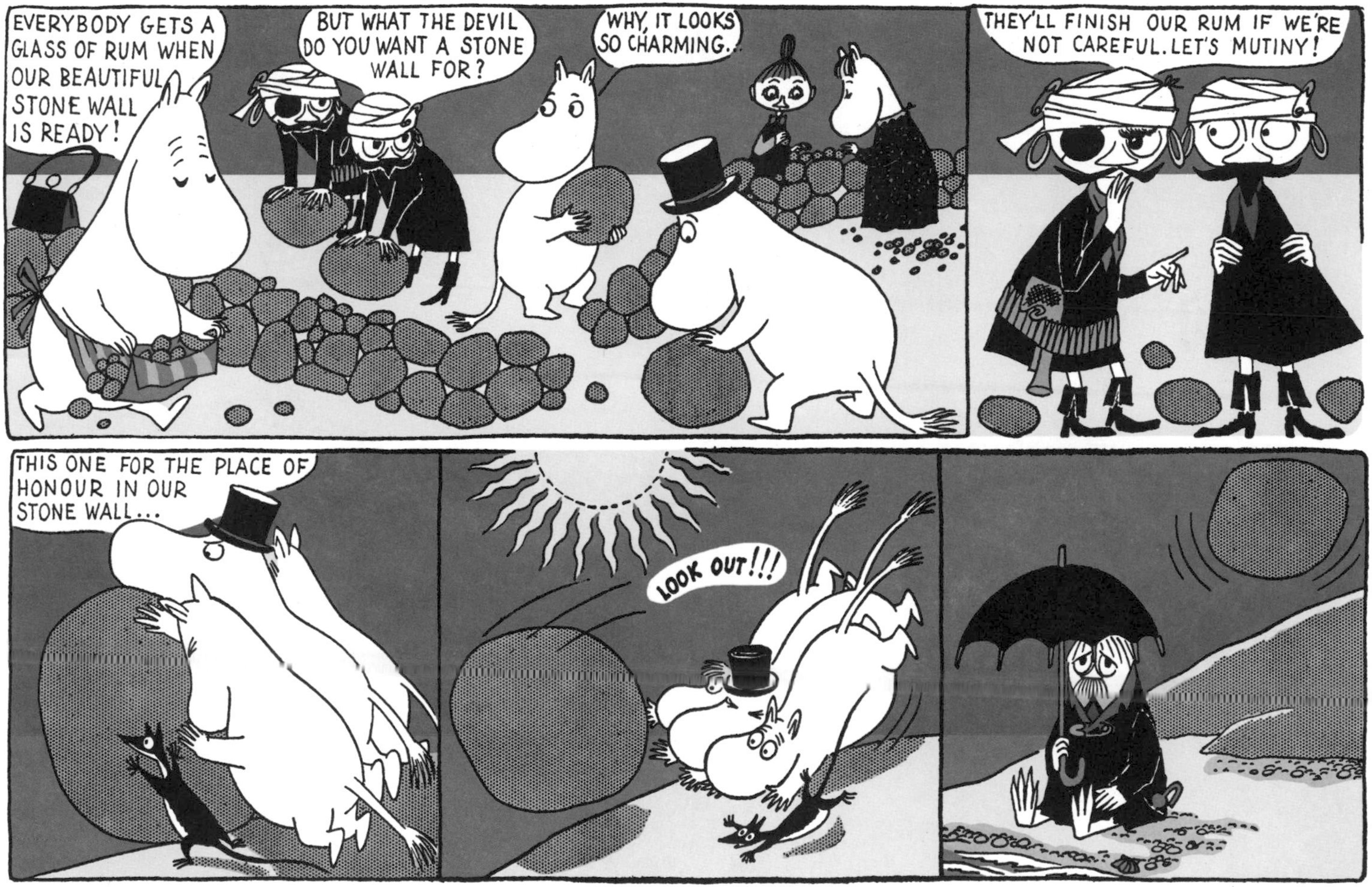
EVERYBODY GETS A GLASS OF RUM WHEN OUR BEAUTIFUL STONE WALL IS READY!
BUT WHAT THE DEVIL DO YOU WANT A STONE WALL FOR?
WHY, IT LOOKS SO CHARMING...
THEY'LL FINISH OUR RUM IF WE'RE NOT CAREFUL. LET'S MUTINY!
THIS ONE FOR THE PLACE OF HONOUR IN OUR STONE WALL...
LOOK OUT!!!

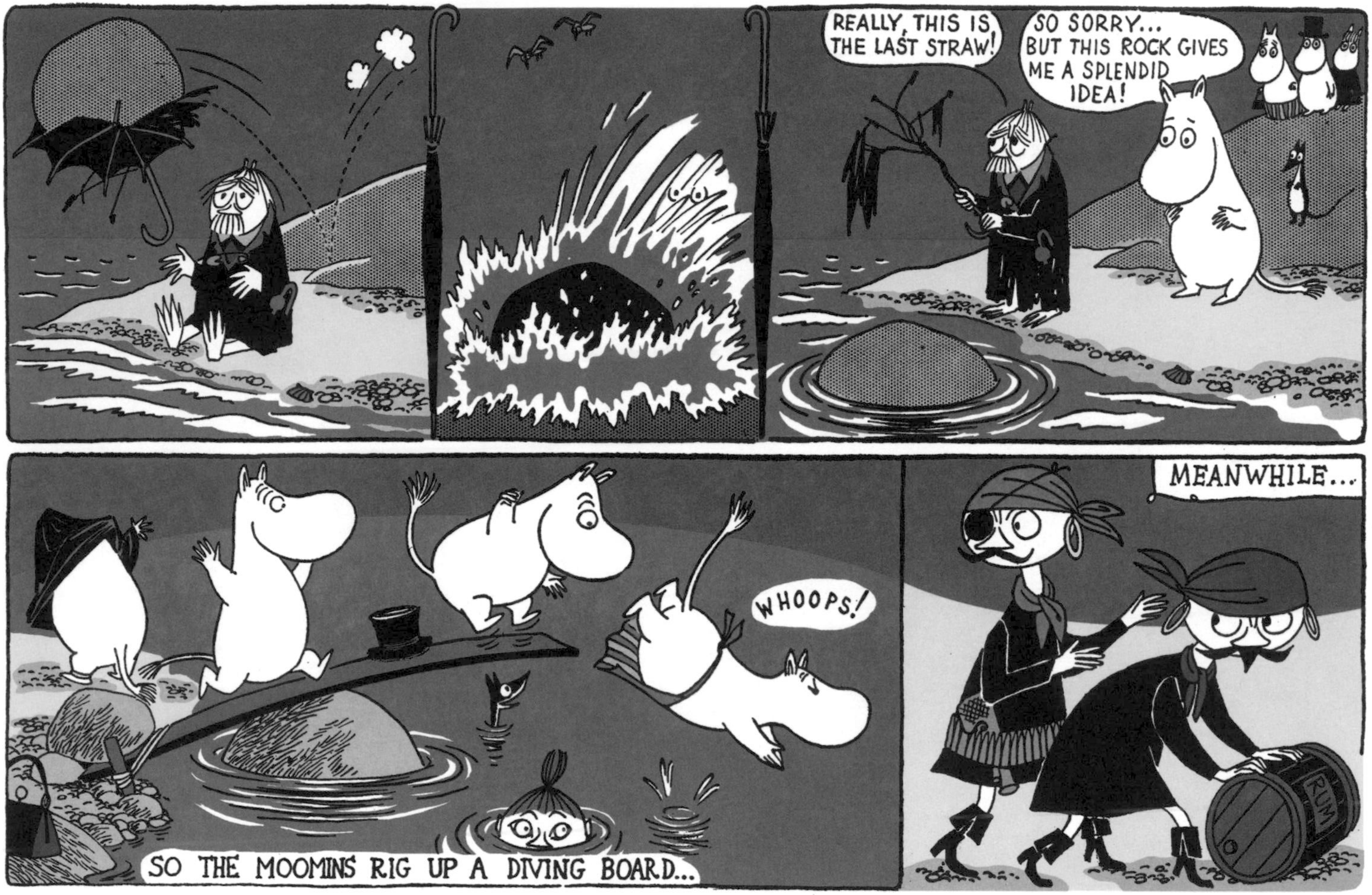
REALLY, THIS IS THE LAST STRAW!
SO SORRY... BUT THIS ROCK GIVES ME A SPLENDID IDEA!
WHOOPS!
SO THE MOOMINS RIG UP A DIVING BOARD...
MEANWHILE...
RUM

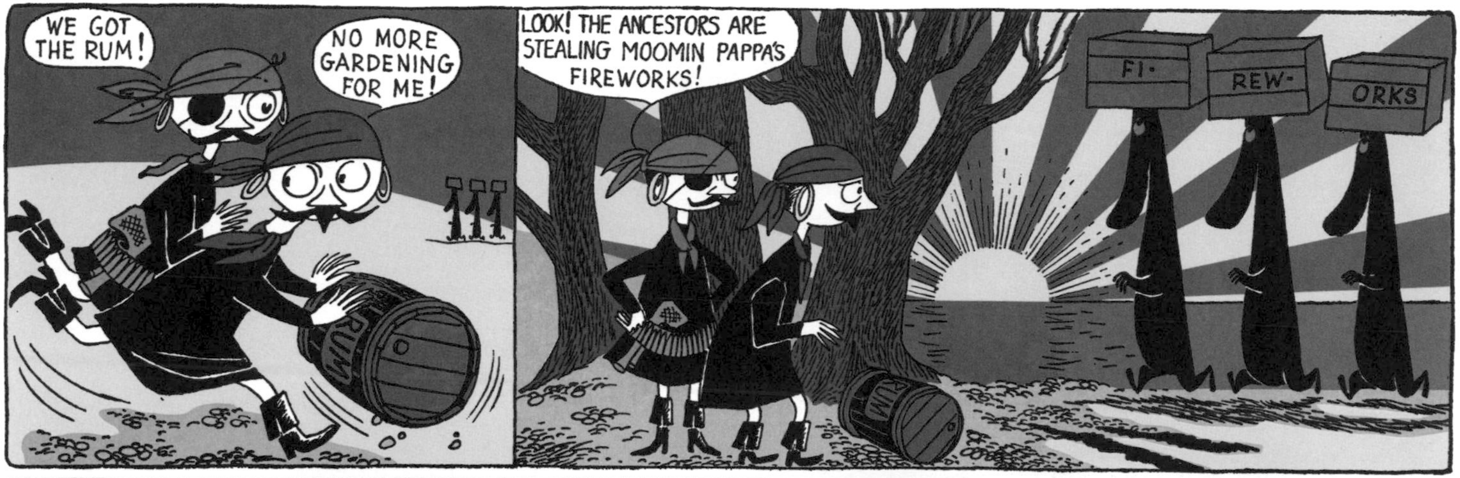
WE GOT THE RUM!
NO MORE GARDENING FOR ME!
RUM
LOOK! THE ANCESTORS ARE STEALING MOOMIN PAPPA'S FIREWORKS!
FI-
REW-
ORKS
RUM

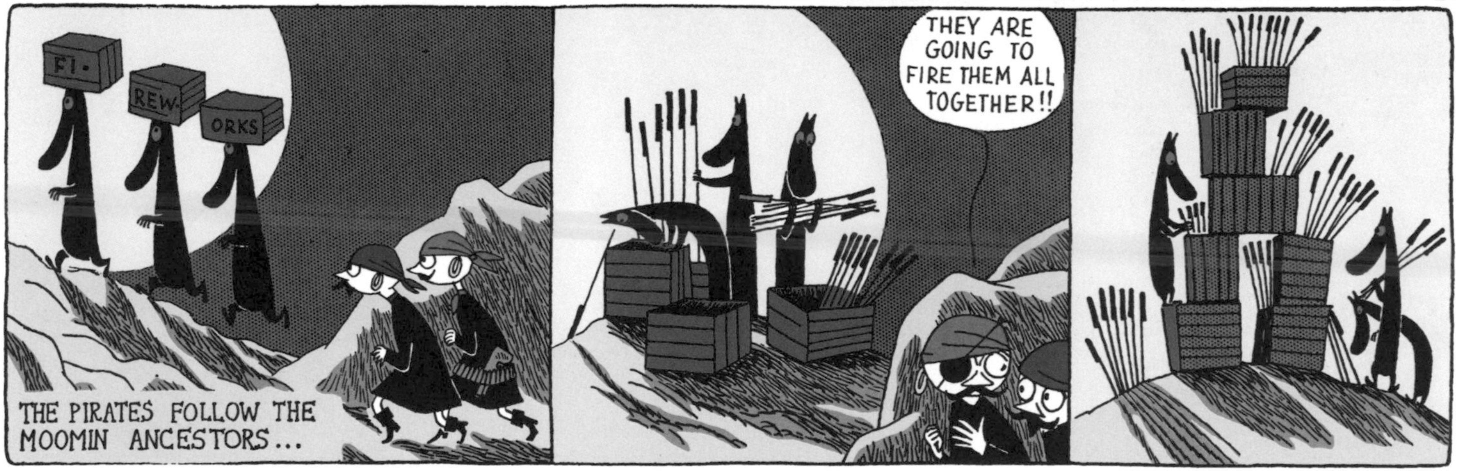
FI-
REW-
ORKS
THE PIRATES FOLLOW THE MOOMIN ANCESTORS...
THEY ARE GOING TO FIRE THEM ALL TOGETHER!!

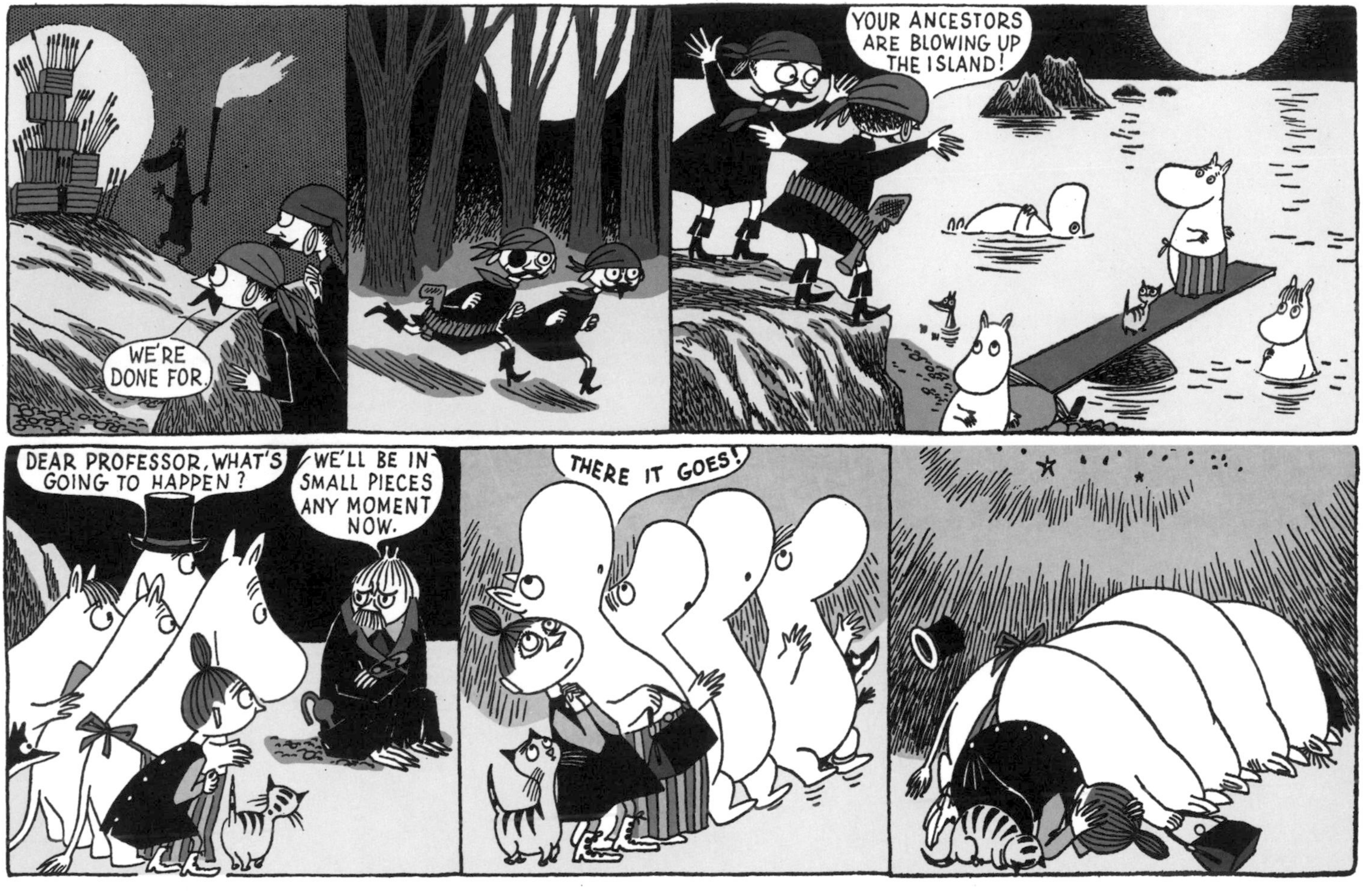
WE'RE DONE FOR.
YOUR ANCESTORS ARE BLOWING UP THE ISLAND!
DEAR PROFESSOR, WHAT'S GOING TO HAPPEN?
WE'LL BE IN SMALL PIECES ANY MOMENT NOW.
THERE IT GOES!

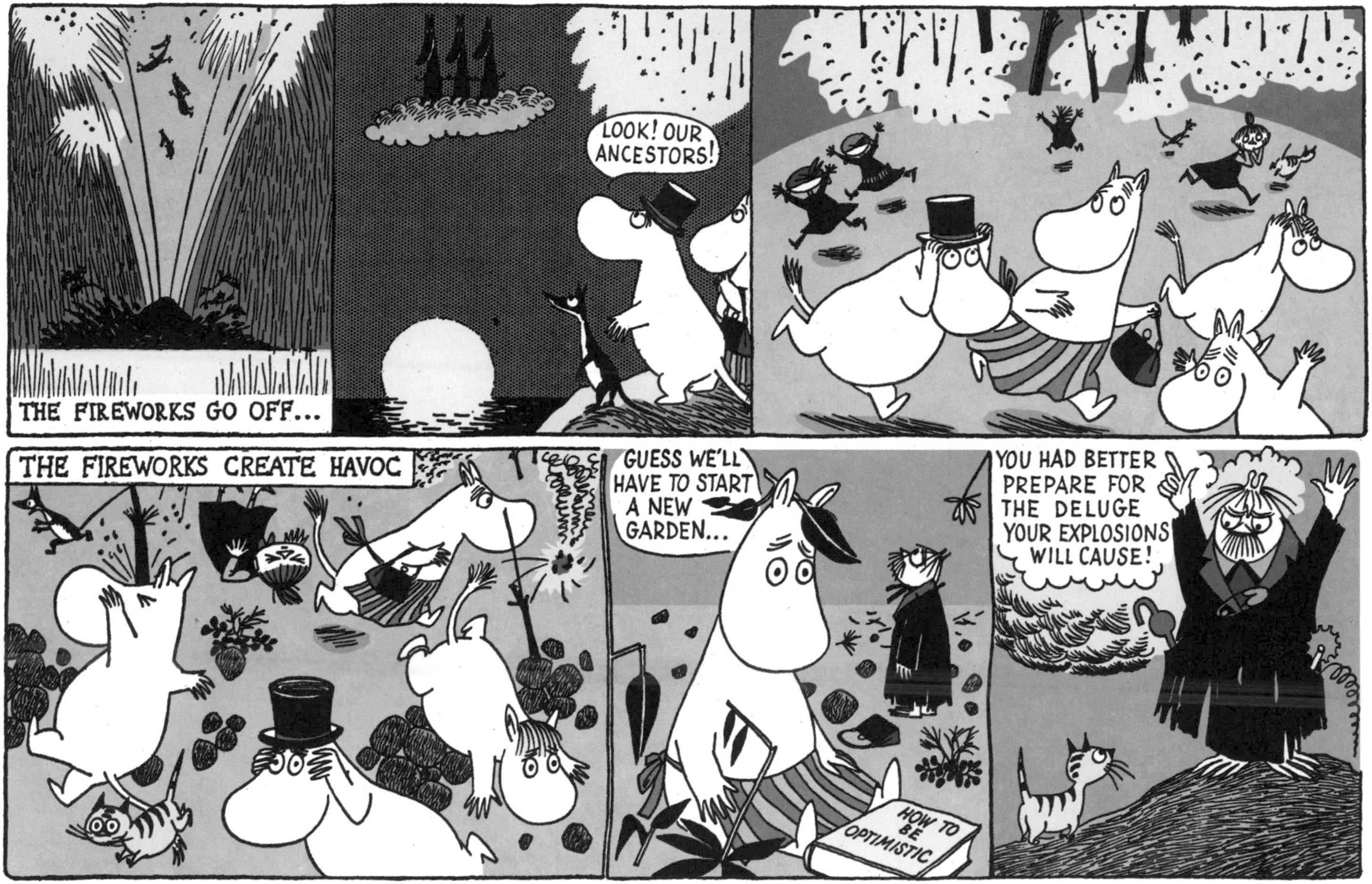
THE FIREWORKS GO OFF...
LOOK! OUR ANCESTORS!
THE FIREWORKS CREATE HAVOC
GUESS WE'LL HAVE TO START A NEW GARDEN...
HOW TO BE OPTIMISTIC
YOU HAD BETTER PREPARE FOR THE DELUGE YOUR EXPLOSIONS WILL CAUSE!

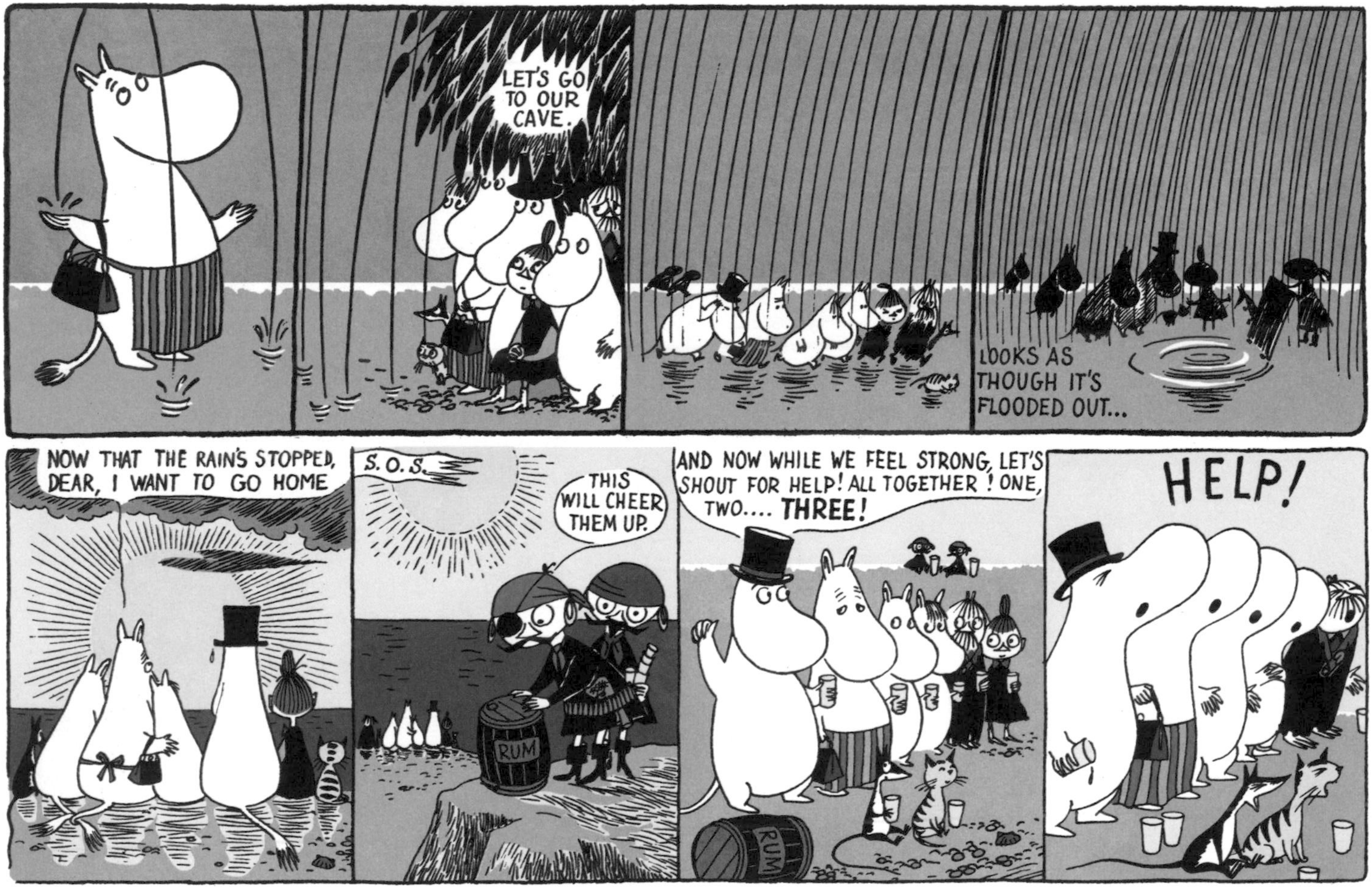
LET'S GO TO OUR CAVE.
LOOKS AS THOUGH IT'S FLOODED OUT...
NOW THAT THE RAIN'S STOPPED, DEAR, I WANT TO GO HOME
S. O. S.
THIS WILL CHEER THEM UP.
RUM
AND NOW WHILE WE FEEL STRONG, LET'S SHOUT FOR HELP! ALL TOGETHER ! ONE, TWO.... THREE!
RUM
HELP!

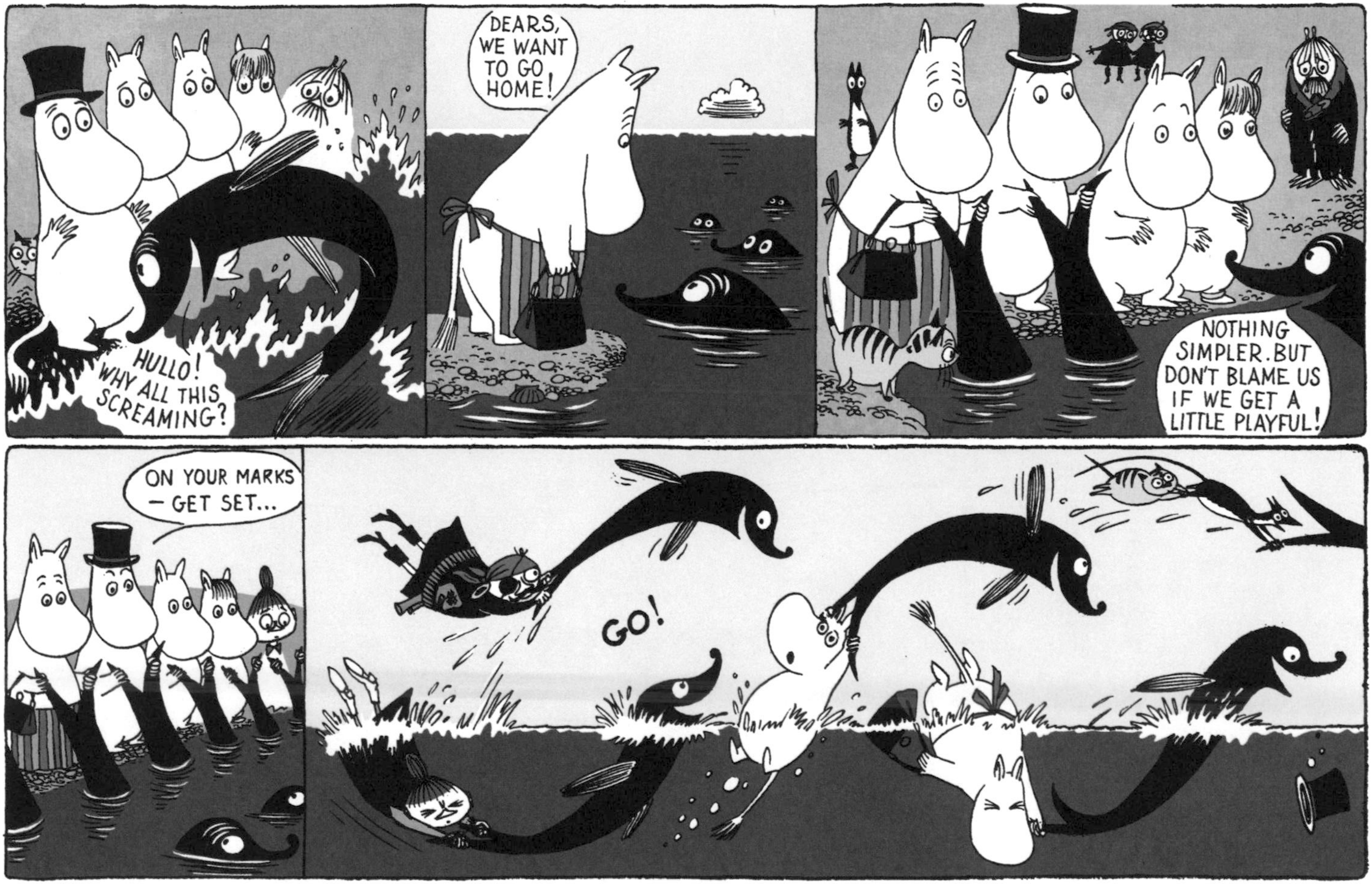
HULLO! WHY ALL THIS SCREAMING?
DEARS, WE WANT TO GO HOME!
NOTHING SIMPLER. BUT DON'T BLAME US IF WE GET A LITTLE PLAYFUL!
ON YOUR MARKS — GET SET...
GO!

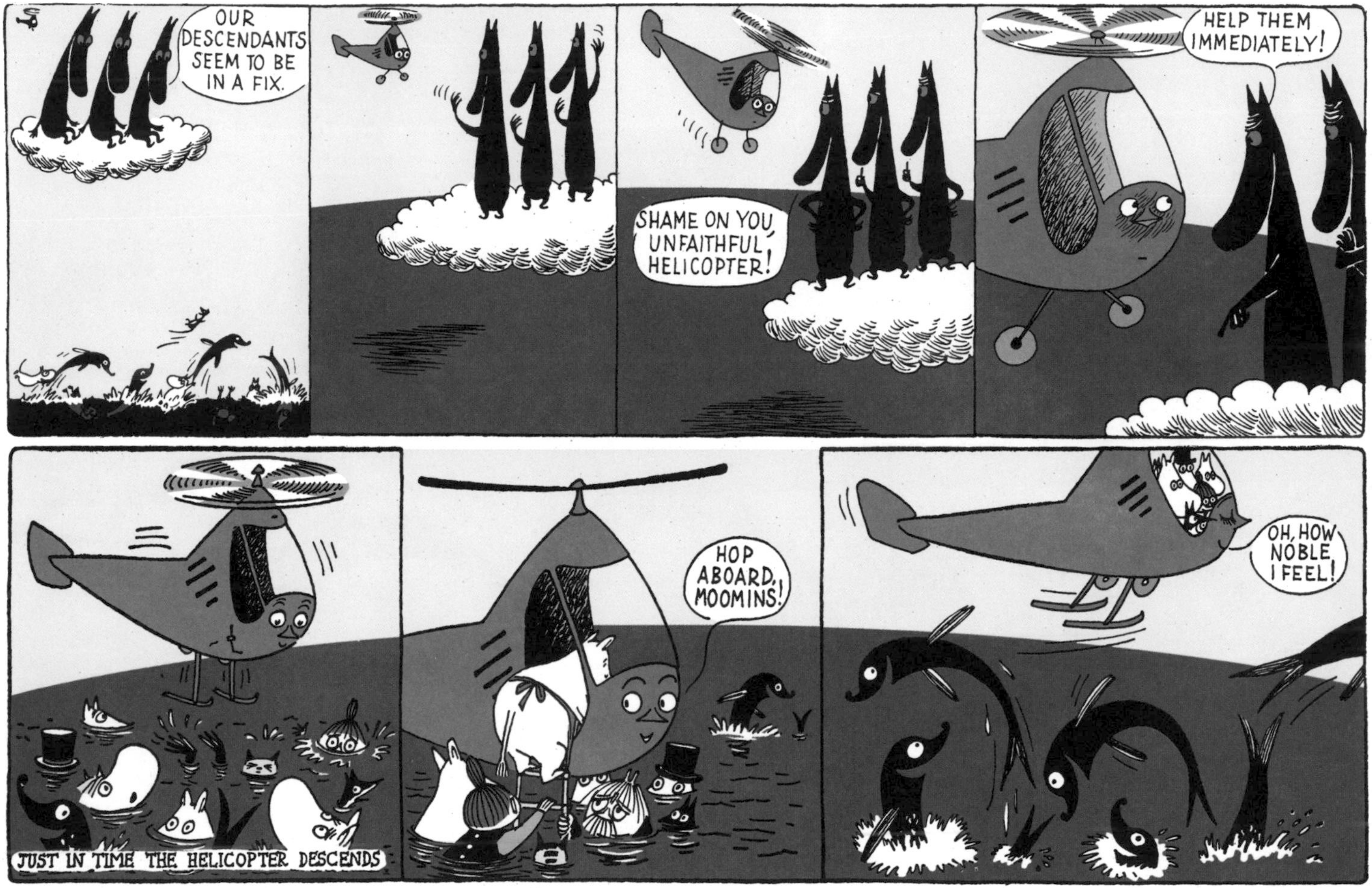
OUR DESCENDANTS SEEM TO BE IN A FIX.
SHAME ON YOU, UNFAITHFUL HELICOPTER!
HELP THEM IMMEDIATELY!
JUST IN TIME THE HELICOPTER DESCENDS
HOP ABOARD, MOOMINS!
OH, HOW NOBLE I FEEL!

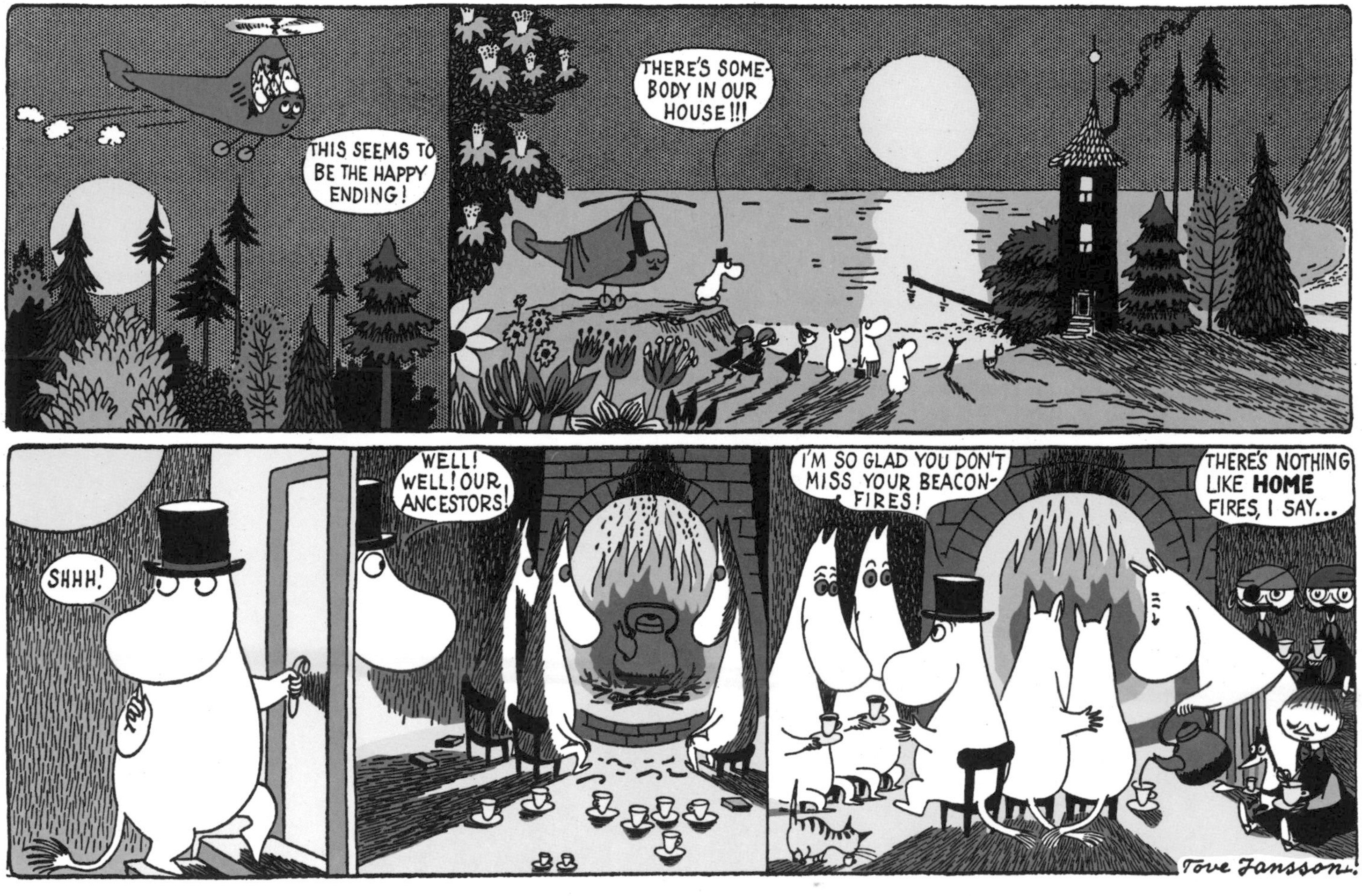
THIS SEEMS TO BE THE HAPPY ENDING!
THERE'S SOMEBODY IN OUR HOUSE!!!
SHHH!
WELL! WELL! OUR ANCESTORS!
I'M SO GLAD YOU DON'T MISS YOUR BEACON-FIRES!
THERE'S NOTHING LIKE **HOME** FIRES, I SAY...
Tove Jansson

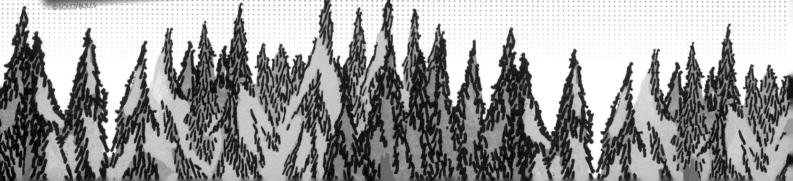

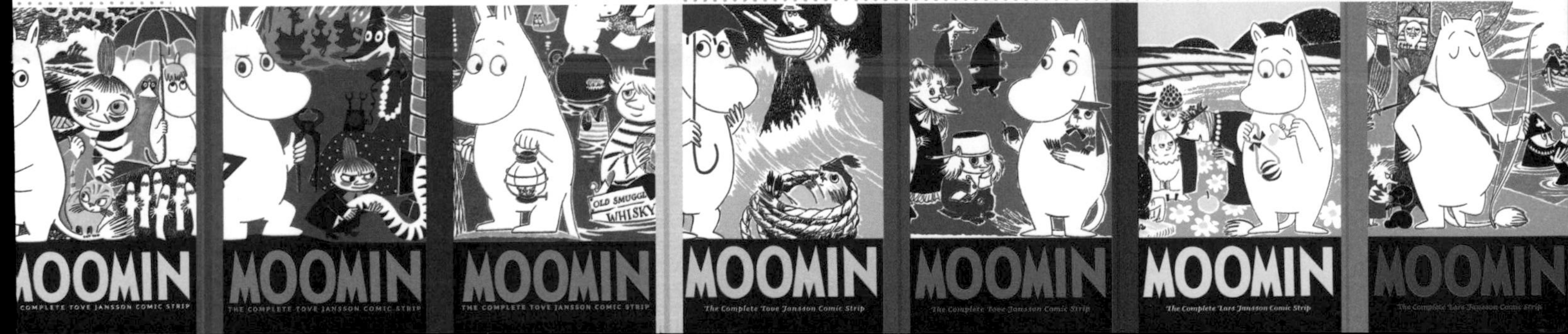
MOOMIN
COMPLETE TOVE JANSSON COMIC STRIP
MOOMIN
THE COMPLETE TOVE JANSSON COMIC STRIP
OLD SMUGG
WHISKY
MOOMIN
THE COMPLETE TOVE JANSSON COMIC STRIP
MOOMIN
The Complete Tove Jansson Comic Strip
MOOMIN
The Complete Tove Jansson Comic Strip
MOOMIN
The Complete Lars Jansson Comic Strip
MOOMIN
The Complete Lars Jansson Comic Strip

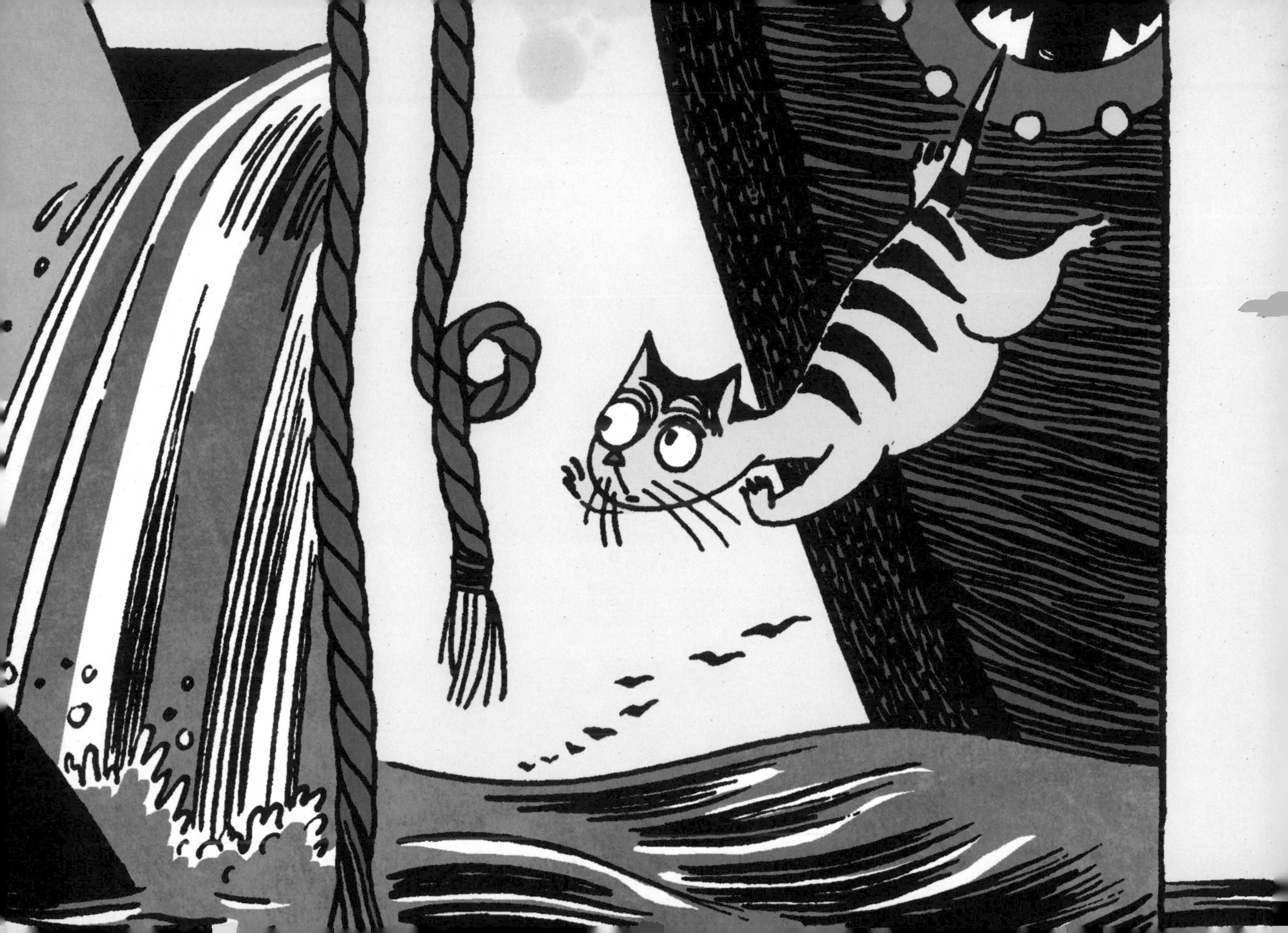

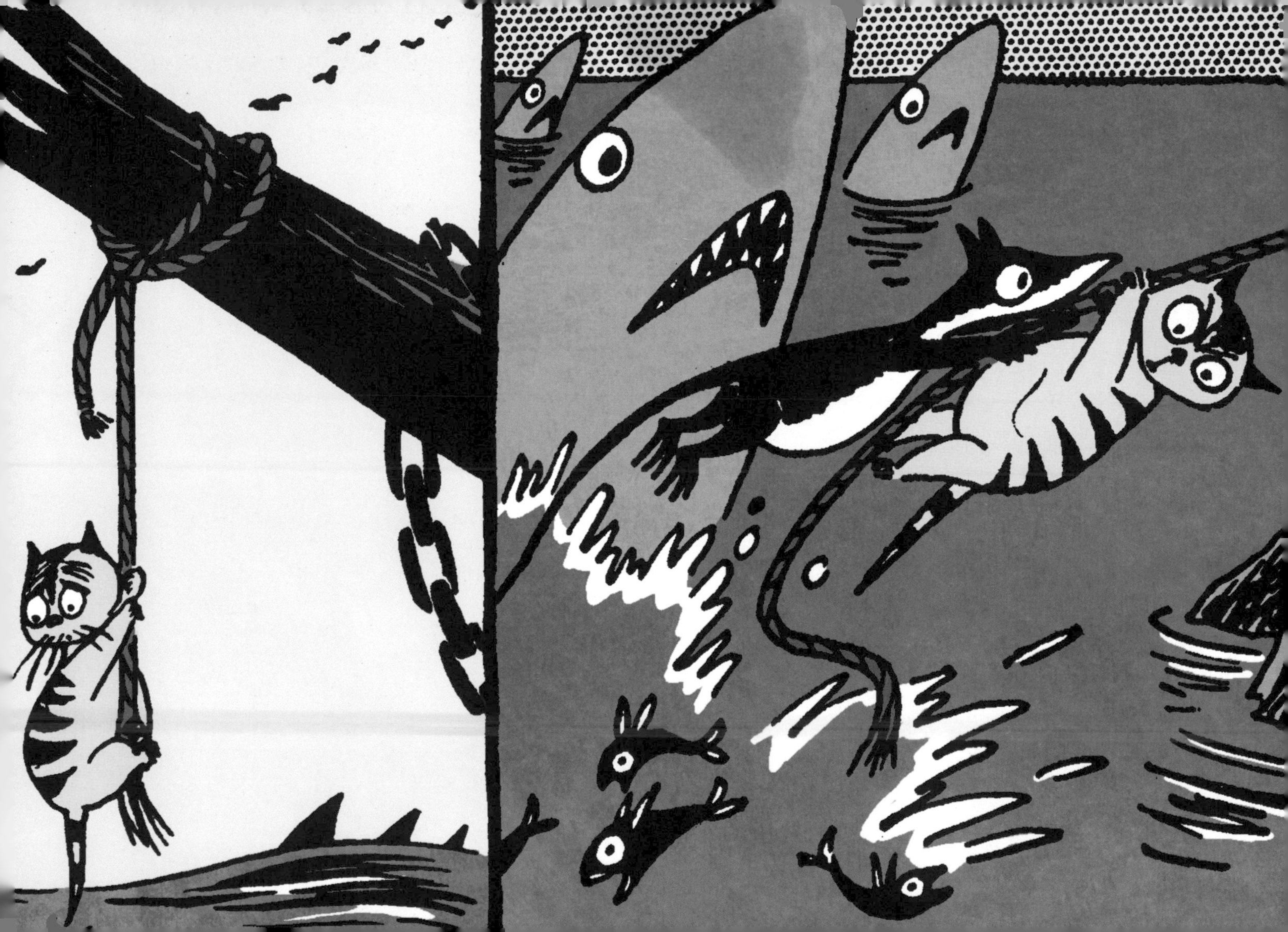

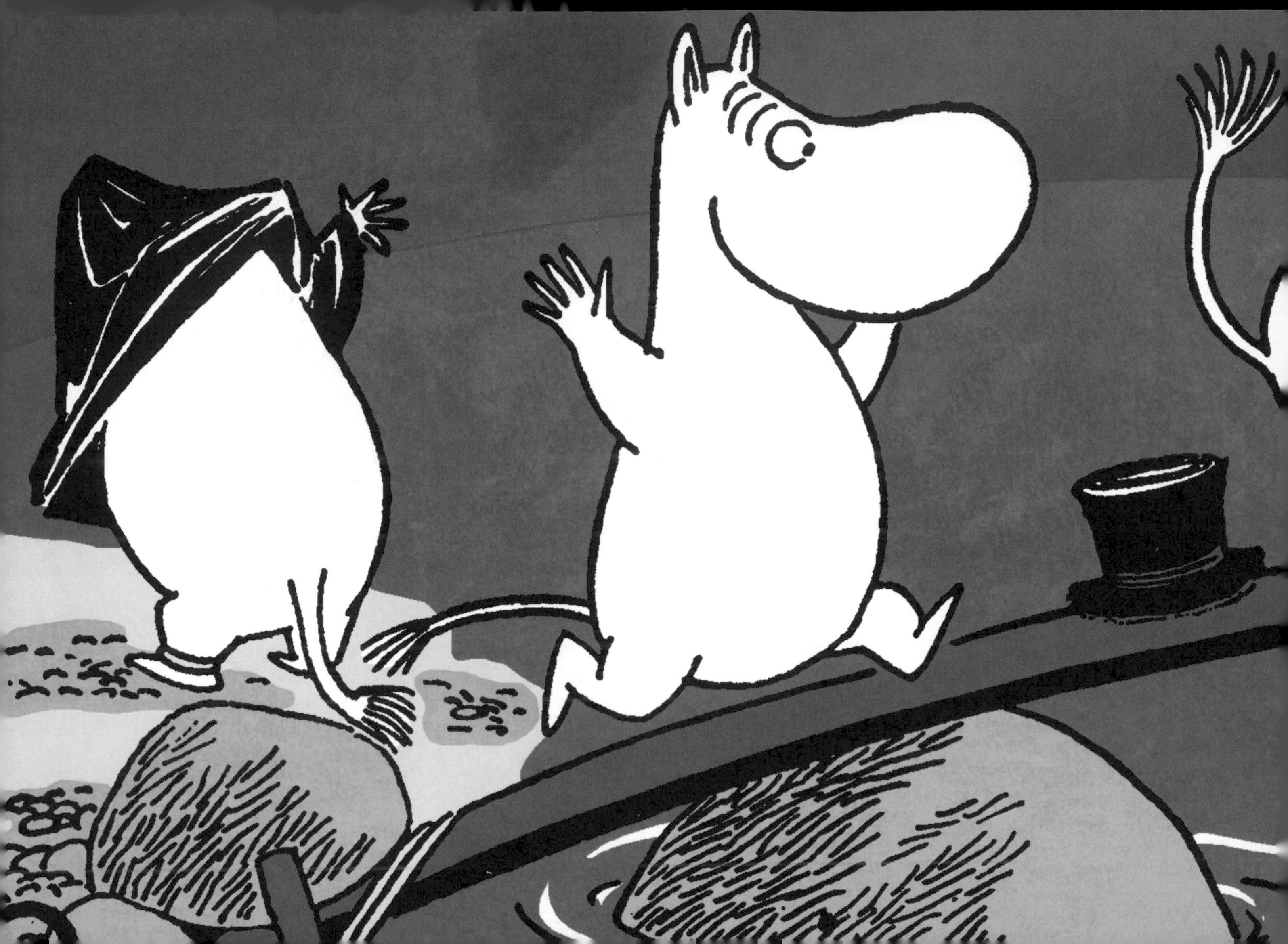

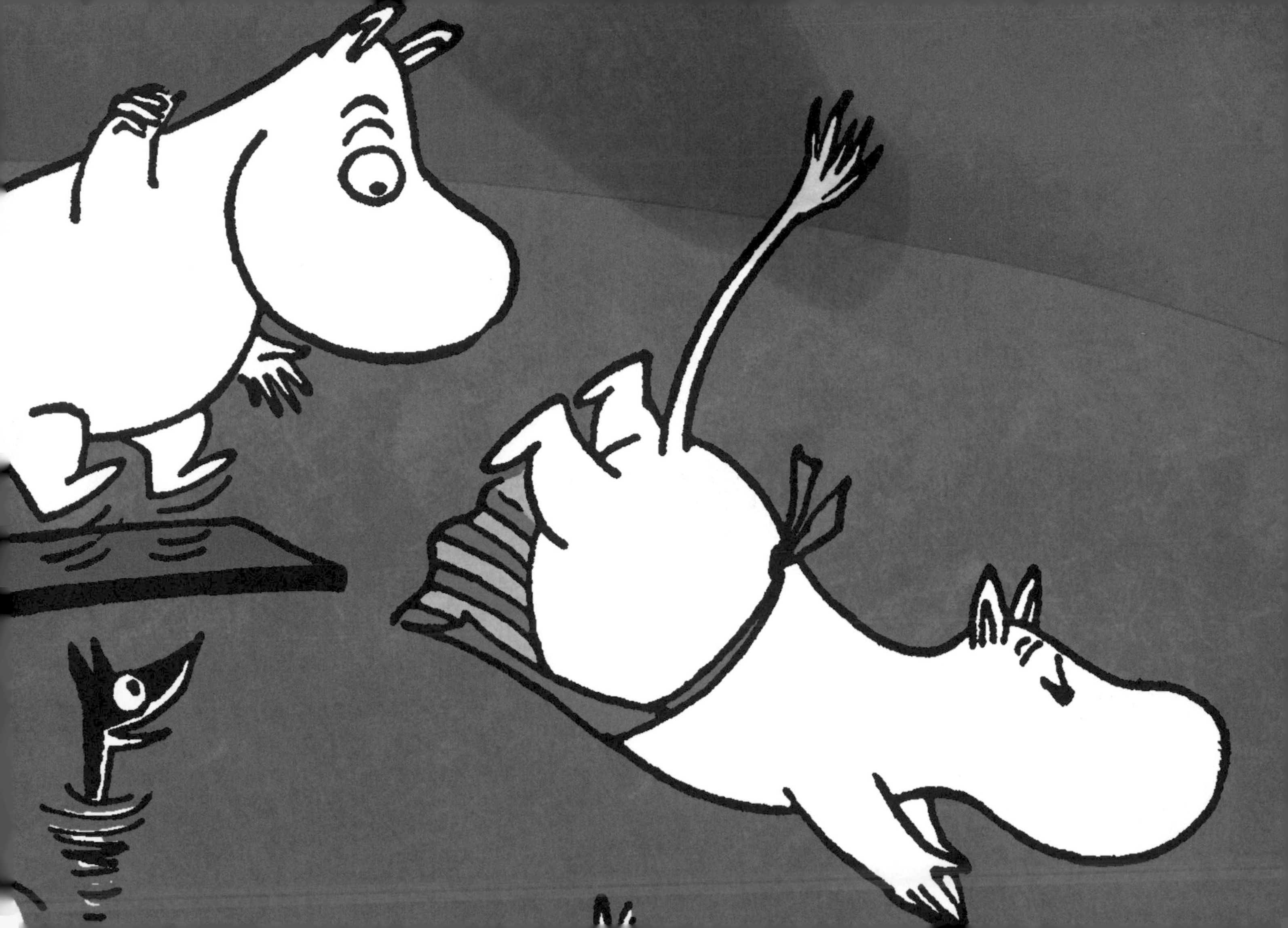

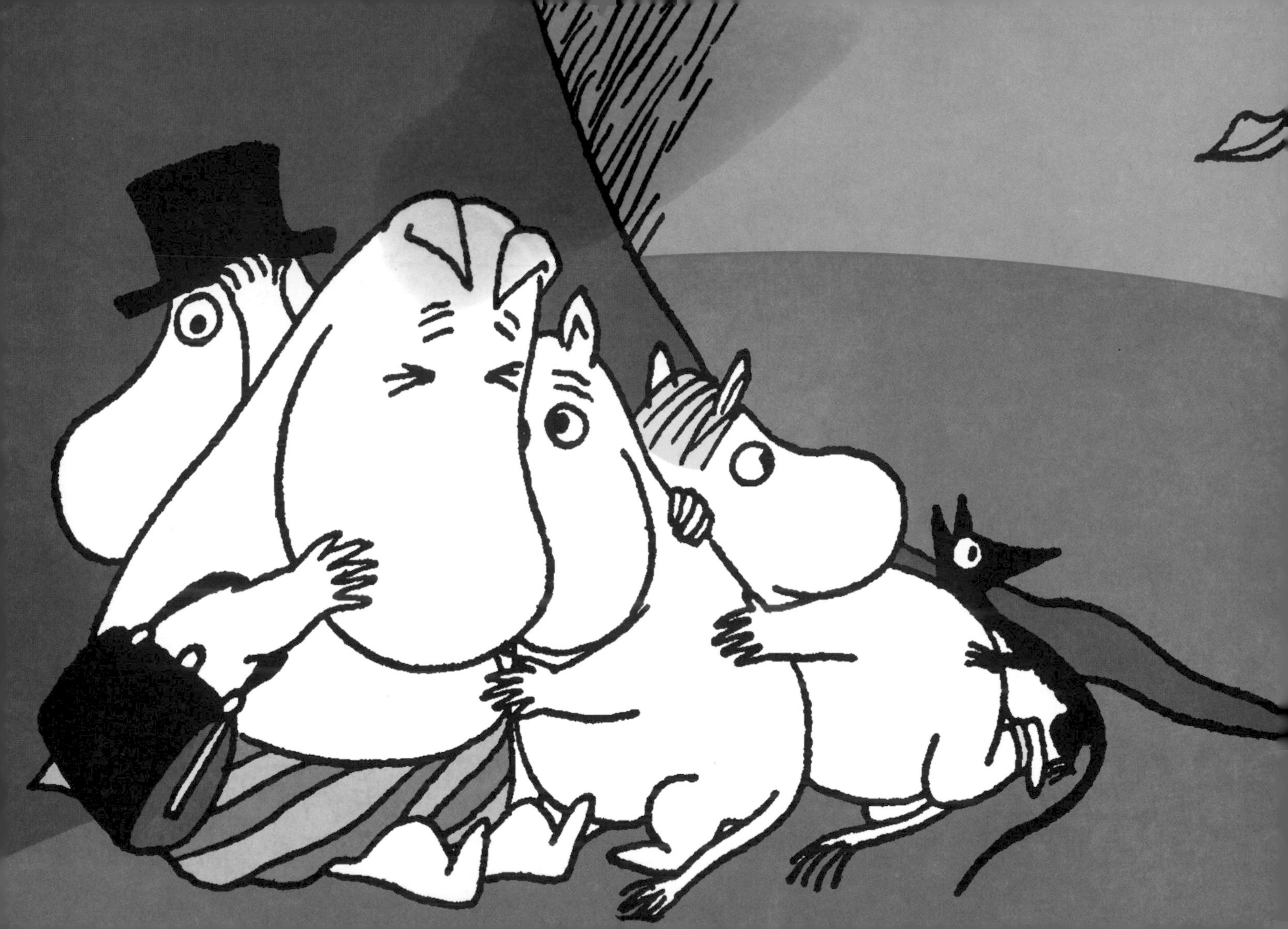

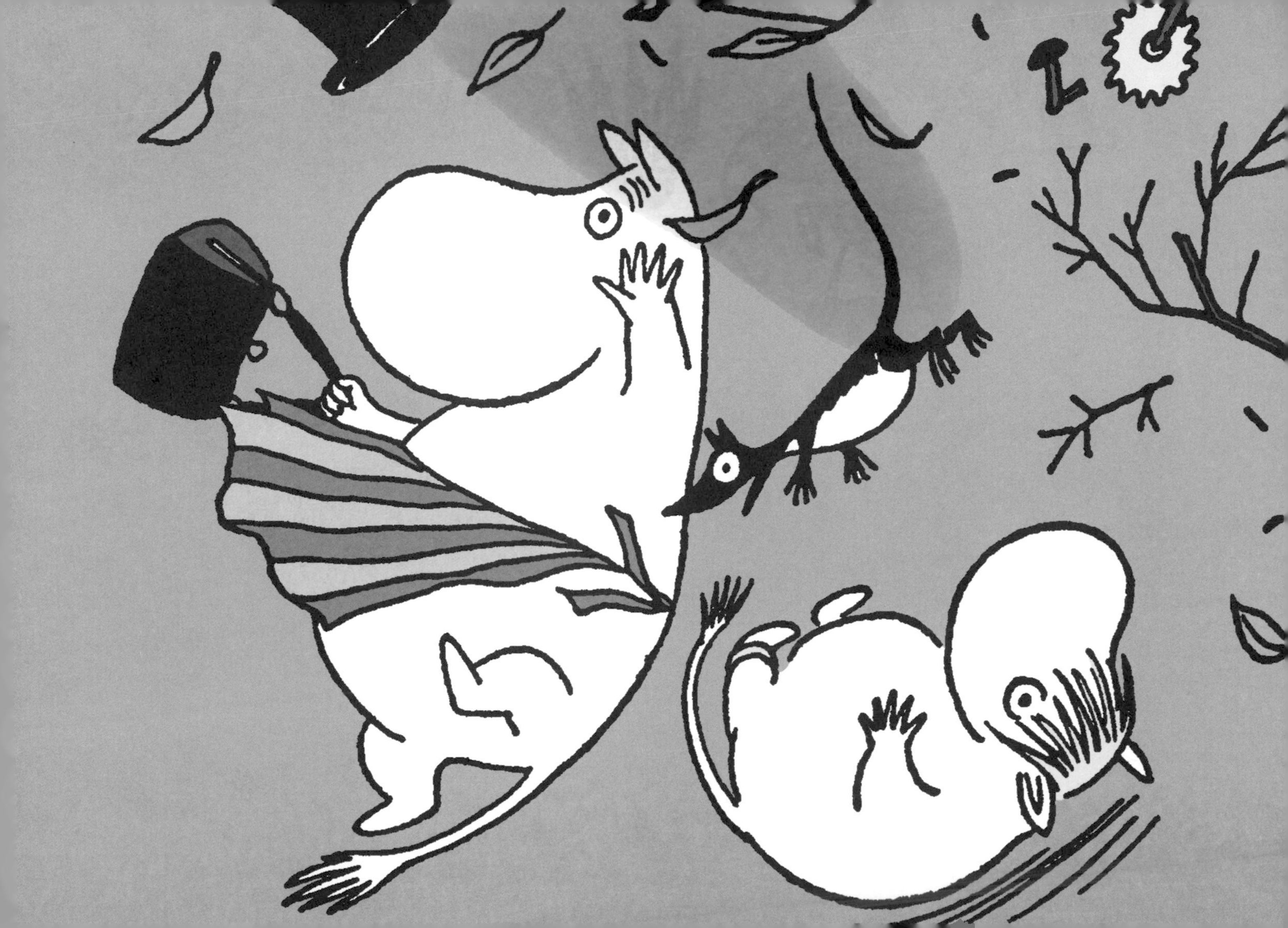

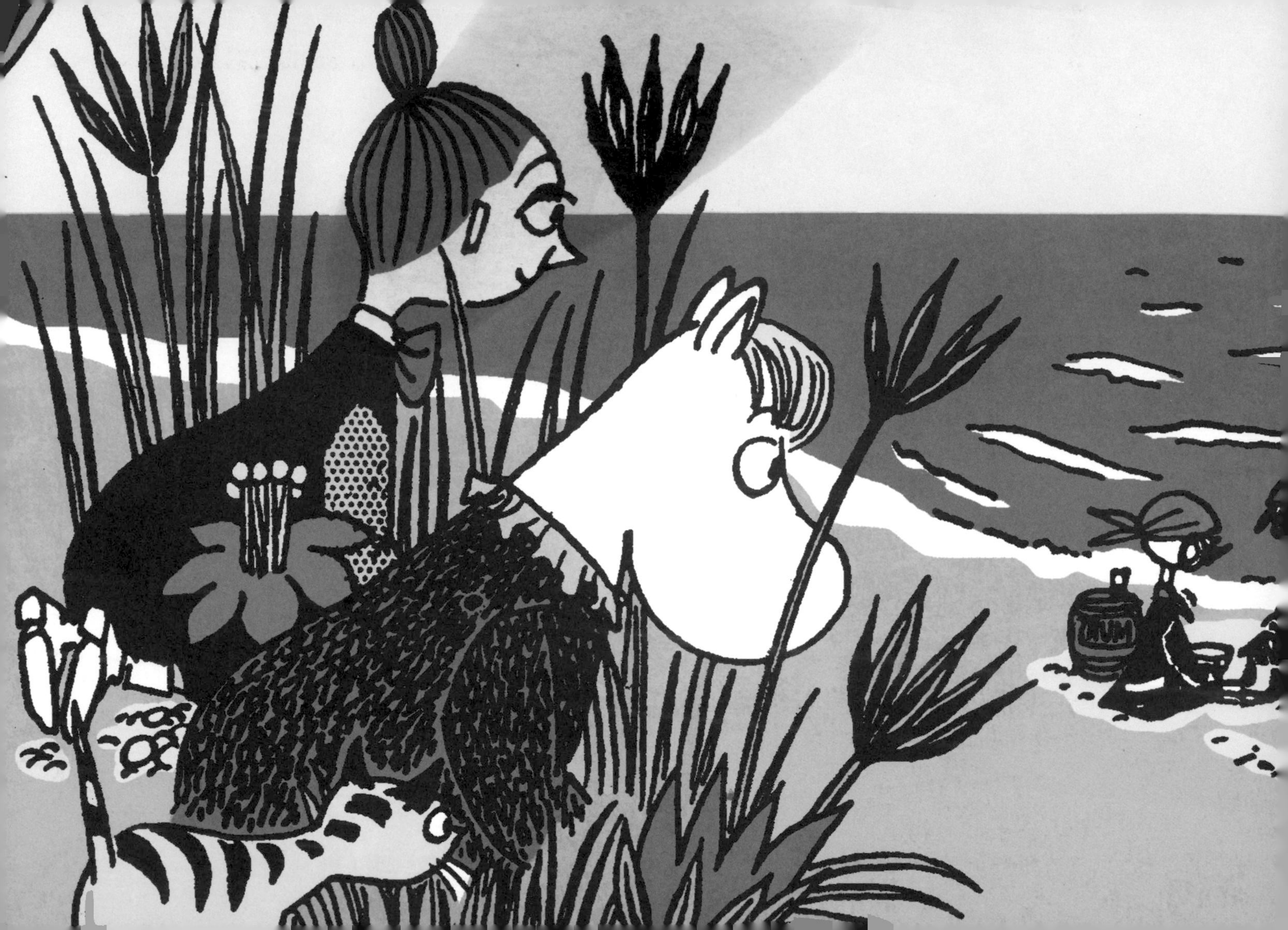